BEING HUMAN BEING

To Gessy and Starr,
Keep up the good work!
Jim (Publisher)
Jan 2024

Being Human Being

Jonathan H.W. Jones

Jonathan H.W. Jones

LYTTON PUBLISHING COMPANY
Established 1975
Sandpoint, Idaho

Published 2024 by Lytton Publishing Company
This book is not copyrighted and may be freely reproduced.

ISBN 978-0-915728-32-9

Senior Editor and design: Rachael Payne, SmartProse.com
Cover design: Doug Fluckiger, Silver Creek Studio

Lytton Publishing Company
Box 1212
Sandpoint, ID 83864

For more information,
visit www.LyttonPublishingCo.com

1

There she was again, down there in the park on the same bench as yesterday. Looking from my second-floor office window, I could see her clearly through the leafless branches. New York's grim cold and slush had now become a distant memory. The April air was mild and inviting, and the grass of Tompkins Square had turned a vivid green. Especially delightful was the line of red tulips alongside the walkway where she was sitting. They reminded me of British redcoats from colonial times, standing in their tiny row. But the woman wasn't inspecting this striking little regiment, or basking in the gentle sunshine. She was engrossed in her smartphone, head bowed, eyes intently fixed on the device, her fingertips trilling against the screen.

She certainly was pretty to look at, wearing a bright green blouse that set off her light brown hair. Tight-fitting, dark pants highlighted her slender figure. She seemed very alone.

"Can't take your eyes off her, eh, Jon?"

I pulled back in surprise, a little embarrassed that Asher had crept up behind me and was reading my mind.

"I'm just kidding," he said with a smile. Then, peering down at the park, he added, "Actually, she's not bad looking."

Asher McClure is my boss here at Ringo Listings, the real estate marketing firm where I've worked as a writer for the past four years. For the most part, it's a fairly mechanical job. We're middlemen in the real estate sales and rental business, collecting listings and farming out ad copy to print and digital outlets. We invent clever ways to describe run-down office suites and dingy apartments to make them sound attractive to buyers. For years, our office had been in a 34-story building on 77th Street, but just four months ago, Asher had moved us downtown to this remodeled brick tenement on E. 10th Street, overlooking Tompkins Square Park near Greenwich Village. When I asked why we moved to the Village he said, with a twinkle in his eye, "I thought it would be nice to get back to nature." This comment didn't make much sense but I let it pass. I assumed the real reason for the relocation was probably a better price on the lease. But, as a matter of fact, moving into this old building on the square did put us next to some trees and flowers—and park benches on which sat young ladies in tight-fitting pants.

"It's a nice day out there," I said, trying to shift attention to generalities.

Asher ignored my evasion and continued to examine the figure on the bench, standing erect by the window in his neat blue blazer, (Asher is probably the best-dressed office manager in New York). "Poor thing," he said. "She's so totally captured by that phone in her hand. Look at the beautiful spring day out there!" he said, waving his arm at the park. "Those elms, those red tulips, those two mothers with their toddlers ambling in front of her. She isn't paying any attention at all!"

He makes this kind of point about every other day. Asher has this theory about what he calls "psycho-kinetic distraction." His idea is that electronic devices like television and, especially, smartphones, where your fingers are constantly at work, soak up time and attention in a way that ends up leaving the person deprived of normal human engagements. And—according to his theory—this kind of deprivation leaves the person unhappy. I'm not sure I see it that way. It seems to me that electronics are just another kind of activity, that they can add to life. And anyway, we don't want to go back to the stone age, do we?

I do have to hand it to him: he does practice what he preaches. Although Asher has a cell, he leaves it at the office. And he doesn't have a television at home, as I'm reminded when some big national news event happens and he doesn't know about it the next morning. In fact, he didn't even know who won the presidential election the morning after—this was last November. "Who wants to know that stuff," he said to me after I told him the outcome and chided him for not keeping up with current events. "It's all a game. Two months later, people forget that it even happened." Asher has a very negative attitude toward politics.

He certainly has been a good boss, in terms of making assignments and letting me adjust my schedule. Last fall, he let me have three weeks off for my Great Wall expedition. Of course, he does tease me about my shyness—which is sometimes deserved. It's true, I don't push myself to meet other people. I feel uncomfortable about it, that's all. I don't like to intrude into other people's private lives, just like I don't want people to intrude into mine. I think it's rude to stare people in the eye.

I felt I should make some kind of reply to Asher's observation about Miss tight pants down in the park. "So your idea is that she's unhappy?"

He continued to stare at her. After a pause, he said, quietly, "Could be."

"But, I don't think that's. . . necessarily true," I said. "I mean, you can't always tell by looking at someone how happy they are. I agree she's engrossed in her phone, but she could be in seventh heaven, texting some romantic Hungarian count about his proposal of marriage." Asher continued staring out the window, saying nothing. Then, suddenly, he turned to me and slapped his hand on the desk.

"You want to bet?"

I looked at him, puzzled.

"I don't mean about the Hungarian count," he continued. "I mean about her being unhappy." He sounded quite serious. I let my gaze shift away to the window.

"Well, uh, how would we settle such a bet?"

Asher rubbed his chin. "Difficult, isn't it?" he said, murmuring more to himself than to me. He stood there in his neatly-pressed slacks, staring down at the figure on the bench, thinking hard. After a few moments, he let out a big breath and spoke.

"Okay. How about this?" He poked his finger in the air. "The object of the bet is, you get that girl to stop using her phone for one entire day. If you succeed, I'll give you"—he paused—"one hundred dollars!" He let the presumed power of this staggering sum sink in. "Then, in whatever way you deem fitting, you can decide if she was happier on the day without the phone, than on other days. And I'll accept whatever method you use to decide the point." He gave a 'so there!' nod.

"That's the weirdest bet I ever heard," I said, laughing. "And I have to give you $100 if I fail to get her to do without her phone for a day?"

"No, no," he said. "That wouldn't be fair, because that would be a really difficult thing to accomplish. People are really attached to their phones nowadays. No," he said firmly, "it won't be a bet. It's just an offer. If you get her to stop for a day, you get the $100. If you don't, you don't owe me anything. And the happiness question is just a side issue. Something to figure out later."

He straightened and headed for the door, then turned back, and added with a smile, "Anyway, it's a challenge for you to think about."

I expect he was alluding to my rather limited private life. It was true: I had drifted into quite an unproductive and detached existence for some time now. When I graduated from Wesleyan University nine years ago as an English major, I had big ambitions as a writer. My roommate in my senior year, Pete Walder, used to tease me about it whenever he found me writing at my desk—it would probably just be a history report or some other homework I was working on—but he would say, "Writing the Great American novel, eh?" This wisecrack didn't bother me, because I assumed it wasn't far from the truth. I admired writers and was planning to be one, and I had communicated this intention to others around me.

This ambition got started back in third grade when, at the encouragement of Miss Blace, my teacher, I submitted a story I had written to the *Daily Tribune*, the town newspaper. It was published prominently opposite the editorial page, and I became an instant celebrity. Friends and relations raved about it. "Frank Frank." That was the title of the story. It was about a man who always told people what he thought about them, criticizing them, and they finally got mad and ganged up on him, disagreeing with everything he said. That turned him around, into becoming a person who praised and complimented everyone. "How could a person so young have so much talent?" said Uncle Mort.

Miss Blace brought copies of the newspaper and passed them around the class. (I think part of her enthusiasm came from the fact that the clever title was her idea—as was a lot of the plot). For a few days thereafter, my classmates spoke to me in quiet, respectful tones, and kept a slight physical distance from me, as if my body had some kind of electrical charge. After that experience, I knew what I wanted to be when I grew up. Other boys wanted to be pilots or engineers; I was going to be a famous writer.

I finished my first novel the year after I left Wesleyan and sent it to Prof. Davis, the English teacher there I knew pretty well. It was a detective story I titled *Once is not Enough*. "For one thing it's too short," he wrote back (It was 134 pages). "Readers want their money's worth." I've since weighed his point—literally hefting the best-sellers that I come across in bookstores—and I've decided he was on to something. Maybe it sounds silly, but many purchasers seem to apply to books the same notion of physical value that they use when buying steak or bananas. They go for the deal that gives them more weight per dollar. A 400-page book for $20 is a better value than a 200-page book for $18. If you doubt this, consider *War and Peace*. The copy I saw was 1,358 pages long. A person practically couldn't live long enough to finish reading it!

And yet Tolstoy is a world-famous author.

Keeping this point in mind, I've tried to develop ways of spinning things out. For example, instead of just saying, "She was wearing a white dress," I'll expand it to, "She was wearing a white dress with a pink ribbon and gold-trimmed collar, and a silver brooch that her mother had given her for her thirteenth birthday." Tricks like that, which I've been applying to my second novel, *Prisoner of Love*.

While I'm working on the novel at home at night, I do have to earn a living, of course, as some kind of commercial writer. I started out pretty well, with a job as a reporter for *New York Wise*, the shopping news aimed at up-scale buyers. Sure, the newspaper was a free handout, but I was getting a bit known, with my name on a lot of front-page articles. And I did three background pieces for the *Daily News*, as a stringer. (I also sent several stories to the *Times*, but they didn't take any of them.)

Then *Wise* folded, and I was really scrambling. I even worked several months as a stock clerk at Trader Joe's before I finally landed with Asher at Ringo—that was four years ago. It's a good enough job, but, as Asher has said on more than one occasion, it doesn't make history. He's right. Here I am, a would-be writer, cranking out ad copy, leading a pretty boring life, watching too much TV, playing CanyaCong on my smartphone. When I turned 30 this past February, this feeling of drifting really hit me. My life was starting to be over and I hadn't published anything significant. At that age, Mozart had composed most of his symphonies—and he had only five more years to live. When I see my face in the mirror in the morning, I think, *this person is going to die never having accomplished anything.*

The only high points of my life—well, medium points, anyway—have been trips abroad on my vacations. I like to travel to unusual places, and I travel pretty rough, getting to know these foreign lands. I hire an English-speaking guide, for at least a few days, to be able to find out about how the people live, what they think about things. Last year I went to China and hiked the Great Wall: did 51 kilometers! I wrote a little background piece on that, incorporating episodes of my own hike, which *Foreign Adventure* took. They gave me $35.

But aside from my travel vacations, my life is pretty confined. Asher's right: I'm not so good at getting to know people, especially women. I guess you could say I'm a bit shy. I'm not the kind of person who walks up to a woman and says, "Would you like to have dinner with me?" It seems like a simple question, and I know millions of guys ask millions of women that question every day. But it's a hard one for me to ask. It seems so aggressive, so likely to produce some kind of rejection, that I just hold back.

So, given the way my life was going—or rather, not going—I could see why Asher's threw out his challenge. He thinks I need to get out of myself.

My first reaction to his bet—or dare, really—was to dismiss it as just another tease about my shyness. But as I thought about it, glancing again and again at that woman in the bright green blouse down in the park, I thought that maybe I was being a little cowardly. I chided myself: 'Hey, come on, what can it hurt? Don't you even have the guts to walk down into a park and say hello to someone? Let her spit in your face if that's what's going to happen. It can't kill you.'

I had just finished writing the listing I had been working on and it was nearly lunchtime. I decided to try my luck. As I passed Asher's door, I said, "Is it okay if I take a break in the park now?"

Asher smiled knowingly and gave me a thumbs-up. "Good luck."

As I went down the stairs, I considered my approach. How was I going to do this? You can't just walk up to a young woman and say, "I want you to stop using your phone for a day." She'd think I was some kind of pervert. I'd have to move into the idea slowly. I had to break the ice, get to know her. I needed a conversation-starting idea, but nothing came to mind. I was tempted to turn back, but my inner voice shouted, "Go, you coward, for God's sake. Go!"

I walked into the park and crossed over to her bench and stopped at the far end from where she was sitting. She raised her head up from her phone, her delicate brown hair swinging back from her cheek. A small red purse lay on the bench close to her thigh.

"Is it okay if I sit here?" I said, indicating the bench.

"Sure," she said, nodding quickly and moving slightly down the bench as if to make more room for me. She looked back down at her phone, her face serious.

"I wonder where all the birds are?" I said, looking around. She raised her head again and gave me a puzzled look. I was afraid she was starting to think I was being aggressive. I felt I had to explain myself.

"I mean, there used to be dozens of them, starlings mostly, squabbling over bits of bread and stuff." I waved my arm out at the trees. "Now the park is dead and quiet."

She looked over to where I was indicating. "Maybe they've

migrated?" she said. She didn't look immediately back down at her phone, so at least I had succeeded in shifting her attention.

"I'm worried that maybe the pesticides have killed them," I said.

"Do they use pesticides here?" She seemed alarmed.

"You never know." Then after a pause, I added, "It seems there's always something worse happening in the world."

"You can say that again!" she said, shaking her head. She spoke with an air of conviction, like she had spent her life experiencing the world's wars and plagues. Then she looked down at her screen and began tapping on it. In a way, I felt sorry for her. She seemed unhappy, distressed about something and was escaping the pressure of the outside world by retreating to her phone.

I remained seated on the bench, tipping my head back, gazing through the tree branches at the patches of blue sky. After a few minutes, I started feeling embarrassed about sitting there without being able to think of any way to resume the conversation or raise the phone issue with her. I felt it would be too forward to ask her directly about her use of the phone.

I stood up. "I guess it's time for me to get back to work," I said. She looked up and smiled, but didn't say anything. "See you later," I said. She just kept looking at me, open-eyed, smiling slightly but reluctant to say anything for fear of seeming too inviting.

Well, I thought as I walked away, at least I tried. I could tell Asher that I had had no luck and we could just forget about the whole thing.

But as I said this to myself, I realized that would be a lie. I did not actually put to her the proposition about not using her phone for a day. I had been too timid even to bring up the subject.

Dropping the attempt now was simply being a coward.

And besides, there was something about her blue-gray eyes that I liked. They were almost, you might say, inquiring. It was like she wanted more from me but was too hesitant to ask. I didn't want to close the door on a possible connection with her. But how could I proceed?

2

I ran the problem through my mind all that night, tossing and turning in bed, considering lots of different approaches—assuming I saw her there on another day. It was clear that my proposition, if I ever found a way to make it, could be seen as rather insulting. After all, I would be saying, in effect, that I questioned her phone use. You can't just walk up to a stranger and criticize her. You can't say, "That's an ugly hat you're wearing. I'll pay you 10 dollars to take it off." Or, "You have bad posture. I'll give you money to stand up straight." Of course, they're going to take offense; tell you to get lost. I would have to find a way to open up the issue gently.

Well, I couldn't do that until I'd started up a conversation and established a certain degree of rapport. I tried to figure out a way to break the ice. I could say I liked her green blouse—but that could seem like I was making a sexual advance. I could ask her if she worked nearby, or what job she had, but that would be seen as prying. I could say I wanted her to sign a petition against the pesticides that were killing the birds, only there wasn't any such petition.

The harder I tried to invent approaches, the more awkward it seemed. Finally, it hit me. These tactics would all be false! Dammit, I thought, why beat around the bush? Just directly declare my proposition. She'd probably tell me to go to hell, and that would be that. Asher wins the 'bet.' But at least I could tell him I tried, that I wasn't such a coward I was afraid to speak to someone.

I was so eager to have it all over with that I worried I wouldn't see her again. The next morning, the moment I got into the office I looked carefully out over the park. No sign of her. In fact, even though the weather was bright and sunny no one was sitting on any bench in the park. The massive bare branches of the trees hung quietly above the green grass and the red tulips.

I turned my attention to my job, my writing job. Ha! I thought, what a career for the Great American novelist! Writing real estate ads. Of course, I reminded myself, there was *Prisoner of Love*. This was the novel I had been working on in my spare time, for over two years now. It's about a hero who is transplanted in time to an ancient civilization, the Mawah, where they practice human sacrifice. He tries to tell them it's a stupid and immoral custom—and almost gets sacrificed himself. He ends up hiding out in the main temple of the religious sect that runs the country and makes the sacrifices. He's sheltered by—and falls in love with—one of the young priestesses, Darla, who also shares his abhorrence of human sacrifice. I had worked hard to build it up to 176 pages long.

The novel had been finished almost a year ago but I couldn't figure any way to be taken seriously by the publishing world. You've got to have an agent in order to have a chance, and I didn't know anyone. Then, just recently, I had a stroke of luck. At a reunion of Wesleyan alumni living in New York, I met a real, live literary agent, Steve Small. He was quite a bit older than me, really well established in the publishing world. He told me to send him

the manuscript and he would see what he could do. I polished
the story and sent it off. That was two weeks ago. Steve told me
that they generally need about a month with a new submission
to make sure everyone in the office has had a chance to examine
it and come to a decision. Each day now, I've been obsessively
checking the mail, e-mail and phone.

The phone did ring that morning while I was in the middle
of drafting a new ad, but it wasn't from Davidson and Small. It
was Judy with Tellum Associates. She was questioning our listing
of a storefront property on 112th Street that had been leased by a
yoga firm. They were now complaining to her about being next
to a jazz music studio. I patiently heard her out, and carefully
refrained from suggesting that it was their job as the realtors, not
ours, to tell clients about the background of the property.

Finally, she ended the call. I put down the phone and glanced
out at the park again. There she was! Sitting on the same bench,
wearing the same dark pants, but a light-yellow blouse this time.
It was now or never. I grabbed my blazer and headed out. I didn't
even say anything to Asher as I went by his door.

It was another lovely spring day, pleasantly warm. Only a
distant car horn broke the tranquility of the park.

I crossed the street and walked directly up to her. I swallowed
hard.

"Hi," I said, smiling.

"Hello," she said with surprising warmth and familiarity,
looking into my face. She obviously remembered me. Her eyes
were pretty, and welcoming.

Trying to think of a way of starting a conversation, I looked around at the park, at the tulips by the walk, and the lawns, now getting rather shaggy and in need of mowing.

Looking up through the branches, I said, "No birds again."

Her eyes followed my gaze. "I guess not," she replied, smiling. Her tone was one of openness, of invitation.

I sat down on the bench, not too close. "Okay, I have a confession to make," I said.

"Oh?" She looked at me with wide open eyes, smiling. "Am I going to have to report you to the police?"

I smiled at her clever riposte. It was like we knew each other already.

"No, no, it's not a crime that I had in mind."

She nodded, still smiling. "That's good."

I swallowed again. "It has to do with your use of that phone," I said, pointing at the object she held in her lap. "Some people have this theory that people are, sort of"—I looked up at the lacy branches of the elms, hoping some words would come—"well. . . too engaged by these devices, and. . . ."

She interrupted me, speaking firmly. "You can say that again!" She held the phone out in front of her and shook it. "The person who invented these things should be put in jail!"

This surprising remark made my task a whole lot easier.

"Oh? You mean, you think you use it too much?"

"Absolutely!"

"Well, then, why don't you use it less? Put it away for a day, for example?

"I can't! It's like you say, I'm addicted." She shook her head. "If I even let it out of my hand for more than a few minutes, I start feeling anxious. Every time I feel bored or tired, I turn to it, even when I know I shouldn't. It's a craving, a stupid craving." Her face tightened in pain.

"Well, what are you using it for?"

"Oh, I have various online contacts, and we message back and forth, and I also play games, mostly what my phone comes with. Lately, I've been playing this new version of hi-lo solitaire—God it drives me mad! Once I've started it, I'm hooked." She shook her head vigorously, and her light brown hair swayed and bounced along with it. "And then I'm always following news updates, about this shooting, that celebrity divorce, what the Royal Family is up to, all that stuff."

"Do you think this information is dependable? Or helpful?"

"Of course not!" She was surprisingly energetic. "It's just that I. . ." She blinked hard and set her jaw. "For you, for most people, the phone is just a help. You can put it down when you want. For me, it's different. Like I said, it's an addiction, like people have to drugs or alcohol. I'm just, just. . . ." The look of stress on her face deepened.

She set her phone down on the bench beside her. She took a deep breath and made a smile. "I'm sorry. I got a little carried away. So, now," she said, spreading her fingers along her thighs to mark a change in subject, "what was this confession you were going to make?"

"Oh my, what a coincidence! It has exactly to do with your using your phone, well, so much."

"What do you mean?"

"Okay, here's my confession: Yesterday, while you were sitting on this bench tapping on that phone"—I nodded toward it—"I was watching you from that window up there." I pointed up through the branches behind me. "That's my office."

She peered up toward the window. I think I detected a little smile of pride, as I guess any woman might feel, learning that she had been attracting attention from afar.

"And I. . ." This was tricky. It didn't seem right to bring Asher into it. "I thought that it seemed you were using your phone an awful lot, that it was taking away from your ability to enjoy life."

"Duuuuh!" She drew the word out long and emphatically, turning her lips down in a sad look.

"So, I thought, wouldn't it be neat if I could help you use it less. Maybe get you to do without it. . . for a day, let's say?"

She looked at me, her eyes wide. "That is an amazing coincidence, isn't it?" After a pause, she gave a little, sarcastic laugh, then said, "Lots of luck. I've been fighting this thing for years," she said, picking up the phone and shaking it. "My friends and I talk about it. The most anyone has gotten me to stop is for six hours, and it nearly killed me."

She gave another little laugh. Speaking quietly to herself as she gazed across the park, "If you could get me to quit for a whole day, I'd pay you." She paused, as it dawned on her that her jesting words could be taken seriously. She raised her voice and turned to me, "Really!"

"Well. . ." I said, feeling that I had maybe bitten off a little more than I could chew.

"I'm not kidding. I'll pay you," she continued, "One. Hundred. Dollars!" Her head nodded firmly on each syllable.

Waving her phone at my chest, she looked into my eyes. "I mean it!"

3

You could say that from that moment in the park, I became a man with a mission. It wasn't the money—although I was quite floored by the coincidence that both Asher and Niccole had offered to pay me the exact same amount of money for this very unusual challenge. It made it seem that the heavens were aligning behind this project of getting Niccole away from her phone. Here was something that two human beings wanted me to accomplish. And, I guess I should add, there was something about Niccole that drew me. I really wanted to help her find strength to accomplish her own goal.

After she made her "offer" in the park, to pay me $100 to get her to stop using her phone, I accepted. "I would very much like to help you do that—and I don't care about the money. Really!"

I don't know how seriously she took my intention to help her with her phone. But I did get her name and contact information, so I could set something up. Niccole Evenson lived at E. 194th Street. Yes, each day, she had to endure an hour-long Subway trip in from the Bronx to her job on 9th Street, just a block from the park and my office. We spoke a little while longer about what we did. I told her about my real estate writing, keeping it brief, leaving the aspiring novelist aspect of my life for another time.

She worked in furniture development. Her company drew up the plans—designs, colors, wood selections—for different manufacturers, especially two in Thailand. Niccole said it was like creating a work of art, but the designs had to be practical and appeal to the average Joe. This frustrated her because she had some ideas for rather far-out pieces. One, which she showed me several weeks later, was for a chair that looked like a flower, resembling a camellia blossom. "So with these in your living room you can think of yourself as a honeybee, flitting about your home," she explained with a bright smile. She said she didn't even dare show the drawing to her manager.

The rest of the day, after we parted, Niccole's challenge was very much on my mind. I had never given any thought to addictions, much less the idea that electronic devices might be one kind of them. How does one overcome a habit like that? I wondered. Are there drugs you can take?

I looked addiction up on the Internet and shuffled through different sites. There were all kinds of programs, clinics, camps for treating addictions. Mostly for drugs and alcohol. But computer games were mentioned as one kind of addiction. One treatment that I noticed was the idea of positive reinforcement: you give somebody an immediate reward if they stop doing it for a brief time. Like paying them to stop.

On my way from the Subway to the office the following morning, I went by a sign in a window that I passed every day. It said, "Addiction? We Can Help!" It was some kind of psychological counseling or therapy clinic. I had ignored it for all the months I had walked by, but now it was speaking directly to me. I entered the office and crossed over to the counter. An older black woman with long, African-type braids looked up from her desk. "Can I help you?"

"Well, actually," I stammered. "I. . . It's for a friend of mine."

She looked at me inquiringly.

"I was wondering, do you deal with electronic addictions? I mean, things like TV and phones?"

She gave a gentle smile. "No, I'm sorry. Dr. Lyons supports those suffering with chemical addictions—alcohol and drugs." After a pause, she added, "I don't know who handles that kind of thing."

As I headed toward the door, she spoke up again, "Come to think of it, there was an announcement about something like that in the rack. Just a minute."

She got up and went over to a display case by the door that held pamphlets and flyers from different support programs. "I thought I saw something here the other day," she said as her finger moved along the bottom row. "Yes, here it is!"

She pulled out a tan card that had printing on one side. She glanced at it and then handed it to me. "It doesn't seem very helpful," she said with a shrug.

I took the card, thanked her and left the office. Out on the street, I studied it closely:

Is TV an Addition or a Subtraction?
Are humans meant to live, or just to survive?
Modern life is full of ways of filling our brain cells with
empty electrons. Come and discuss ways to make your
life richer and more meaningful. We meet:
Place:
Time:

BHB

The spaces where the place and time of the meeting were supposed to appear were almost entirely blank, with just a hint of black handwriting. Apparently, the announcement was very old, even years old, and the ink of the writing had faded away.

And what the heck was BHB? Was it the name of some kind of support group? When I got back to the office, I put it in the search engine, expecting to find the name, but nothing plausible came up. The closest thing was "beta-hydroxybutyrate," some sort of diet additive that is supposed to help you burn fat and lose weight.

Well, maybe that did involve an addiction, but not the one I needed to fix. These three letters, BHB, kept running around in my head the rest of the day. What did they mean?

I was a little leery about trying to follow up on advertisements for treatments of addiction that came up on the Internet, figuring that half of them would be crooks. I wanted something more concrete, something I could personally investigate. Seeing that rack of flyers and pamphlets in the doctor's office reminded me that at the health food store on 51st Street, where I often shop, I had seen a similar rack. That afternoon, after work, I went by the Good Earth Market before heading to my apartment.

There were dozens of flyers, covering everything from aloe vera for wrinkled skin to goji berries for improving your eyesight and turning your life around. There were also flyers promoting different gatherings—yoga classes, training sessions for therapy dogs, and so on. And then I saw it, a flyer announcing a support group for electronic addiction, this time with the meeting place and time clearly printed:

**Too many electrons in your life—and not enough people?
Come to our support group, NA—Nanoelectronics
Anonymous—and share your experience. No cost, no
obligation.
Place: Wagon Wheel Café 366 E 46th
Time: Friday May 1: 8 PM (after café closes)**

Feeling encouraged by finding such a resource, I carefully
folded the precious piece of paper and slid it in my shirt pocket.
As soon as I got home, I telephoned Niccole and asked if she
would be in the park tomorrow. She seemed pleasantly surprised
at my call and readily agreed to be at the same bench at 11 o'clock.

She was already seated there when I arrived, wearing a long,
loose dress made of gauzy purple cloth. It made her look rather
hippie-like: special, not your usual New York City office worker.
The purple of her dress nicely stood out against the bright yellow
of the forsythia bush behind the bench.

"I've been looking into this addiction thing," I told her after I
sat down beside her. "It's pretty complicated."

"Don't I know it!" she said.

I went on to explain about the support group I had discovered
and showed her the flyer. She studied it carefully. "Well, I don't
know," she said slowly. "Meeting with all those strange people. I
mean, who are they?"

"I would go along with you," I said. "And if we didn't like it, or
the people looked questionable, we could just leave, right?"

"I suppose so," she said.

"We don't have to decide now. It's not until next Friday."

Niccole gave a smile that I took as a tentative 'yes.'

"Anyway, I've got another idea for right now. Do you have a few minutes?"

She looked at me expectantly. "Yes."

"One theory of working on addiction," I continued, "is positive reinforcement. You give the person something she likes if she avoids the addictive behavior for a certain length of time. Got the idea?"

Smiling broadly, she said, "Oh, so you think I can be bought? Well, every girl has her price, I suppose," she giggled, flashing her eyes at me. "So, what is my reward going to be? Candy?" She laughed again. "Or how about alcohol? Yes: one addiction for another!" She was obviously enjoying herself.

I let a dramatic silence build, then I answered, "Flowers!"

It was not a spur-of-the-moment idea. I had been giving this challenge a lot of thought. The important question was: what to offer as a reward? Just like Niccole, what first came to my mind was candy, but then I figured that a slender young woman probably makes a practice of avoiding candy, so that wouldn't be too cool.

The right answer had come to me when I remembered that, while gazing out over the park several days earlier, I had spotted a flower vendor, a woman pushing a grocery cart laden with colorful flowers along the paths. That, it seemed to me, was an obvious reward, especially for an attractive young woman. And this flower lady happened to be in the park now.

"Oh, that would be lovely! But where can we get them?"

I pointed through the trees to the woman and her cart by the fountain. "Shall we go over and make a deal?"

We sprang to our feet, crossed the park with eager anticipation and approached a white, four-wheeled cart adorned with colorful bouquets and potted plants, with a woman standing behind.

"Hello," I said as we walked up. "We're interested in buying some flowers."

She was an older woman, probably retired, and was rather short and stocky, wearing a wide blue skirt covered in front by a white apron. Her face bore an angelic smile, so bright you just had to smile back. "Well, you've come to the right place, sir," she said with gentle mock formality.

I picked up on the playacting. "Well, madam, I would like to know which flowers you officially recommend for this special young lady?" I gestured toward Niccole.

"I see," she said, smiling at Niccole. "Well, it depends on whether she likes pink or blue. These David Austin pink roses are just filling out, and then you have these anemones: the blue is especially bright!"

Niccole stepped forward and smelled each type of flower in turn. "Oh, these roses are divine!" She lit up, caressing the light pink petals.

"Good choice," agreed the woman, "and if you keep them in water, they'll last quite a few days."

I paid for the bouquet, a $4, surprisingly low for New York. Also, the round number seemed a bit unusual.

"Can you keep this bouquet here for us until we walk around the park a little bit?" I asked.

"Certainly. You young people go enjoy yourselves." Her glowing sunshine of a smile spread over us like a blessing.

"By the way, what's your name?" I asked.

"Cliona."

"My goodness, that's unusual. Where does it come from?"

"It's Irish. My mother's family came from Ireland, and she wanted to remember the old country." She paused, then continued, "Cliona was the queen of the Banshees. They're supposed to be a real scary tribe." She smiled.

"Well, I'm not scared of you, Cliona," I said, returning her smile. "See you later."

"She's sweet," said Niccole, grabbing my arm as we walked away.

"Yes, yes," I said. "Now," I turned and looked into her eyes, "we have to conduct this experiment."

"And?" Niccole giggled.

"What I have in mind is, you give your phone to me, and I keep it in my pocket for 30 minutes. We walk around the park, inspecting tulips, looking at the clouds, picking up litter, whatever, for 30 minutes. Then you get your phone back—and the flowers" –I pointed back in the direction of the flower cart— "are your reward for doing without your phone for that time. Do you think you can you handle that?"

If Niccole's happiness was the object of the experiment, I certainly had achieved it. She gave a big smile, immediately pulled her phone from her purse and shoved it into my hand. Then we began to saunter around the park, pointing at this plant and that, trying to figure out the names of them. (Beyond the tulips, we were at a loss).

"And so, you said you do something with writing. Tell me again, what you do?" Niccole asked.

I explained about my job at Ringo, writing real estate ads, how I help properties get sold with a good adjective or two. Then I added, "But that isn't the writing I really care about."

"Oh?"

I tried to figure out how to tell her I was aspiring to be something more as a writer without sounding pretentious.

"Well, I think writing should be more than a mechanical job."

"And what. . . does that mean?"

We walked silently for a few moments. Finally, I said it.

"Books."

She gave me a puzzled look. I went on, "I'm writing a book. In fact, I've finished a book and sent it to an agent."

"No kidding! That's amazing!" I felt a little surge of pleasure at having impressed her. "So what is this book about?"

"It's a romance novel, about a guy who time travels back to the days of human sacrifice."

"That sounds interesting."

She was being polite, I could tell, being unable to visualize anything from my compact summary. But I knew that trying to explain further would get too complicated. "Any day now the agent is going to report back about publication."

"Oh, that's exciting! I want to be the first to read it!" She looked into my face with a glowing smile.

After 30 minutes of sauntering—I had checked my watch very carefully—I declared the test period complete. Smiling and laughing, we made our way back to Cliona's cart and claimed the roses. Niccole put her nose against the blooms. "Oh, they smell heavenly! Thank you, thank you," she said to Cliona, who was beaming with delight. Then Niccole turned to me, speaking more seriously, "And thank *you*!"

We bade goodbye to Cliona and walked to the edge of the park where we were to part, and I gave Niccole her phone.

"You know," she was speaking quite seriously, "this reinforcement thing of yours may be working. Usually, when this phone"—she lifted it up in front of her face—"is out of my hand for more than a few minutes, I feel anxious and really want it back, and getting it back again gives me a feeling of, well, release. But now," she looked at me, "now I have very mixed feelings about it. I still feel I want it, need it, but, it feels. . . ." She rubbed her thumb across its surface, "a little dirty, too."

She looked at me with a bright smile. "I think you've accomplished something!"

We agreed to meet in the park in two days, Thursday at 11, for another episode of reinforcement therapy.

Back in the office, I thought about what was happening with Niccole. Sure, I was playing advisor and therapist, but I was also starting a kind of relationship. In fact, I had exchanged more words with Niccole in the past two days than I had with any woman in the past eight years.

Sometimes it almost seems that my brain wants to treat women as fairies in twinkling blue slippers, distant people not to be touched, or touched at your peril. I find them attractive, mind. But when it comes to getting to know them, that's a different story. I don't know why I'm so uncomfortable about having close, physical contact with women. It certainly showed up pretty early in my life.

It might have been set off by Aunt Deborah, my mother's older sister. Debbie, as we called her, insisted on hugging me at the end of every visit before she would leave—she lived in Tenafly, half an hour from our home in Englewood, New Jersey. Looking back on it now, I guess you could say she didn't respect my space, but that is unfair. Debbie was a very loving and considerate person in all other ways. She always gave me the best Christmas and birthday gifts—her Lionel train was my first really significant Christmas present—and she always brought scrumptious prepared dishes to family dinners. And you could say that her eagerness to hug and kiss me goodbye was an expression of this loving spirit.

I remember these episodes quite clearly. There she was, rising out of her chair, all dangling necklaces and tinkling bracelets. She was a big woman, perhaps a little overweight. "Come, Johnny dear. Give your auntie a hug." I'd shrink back, she'd reach out and grab me, I'd squirm and push at her, and she'd manage a bit of a hug, along with kisses on the top of my head. This practically became a ritual. She and my mother would laugh at what they saw as cute, childish resistance on my part. However, at about age 8, there came a turning point. I was resisting and pushing as usual and Aunt Debbie dropped her arms, stepped back and said, "Well, if that's the way you're going to be, I am never going to hug you again!"

And she meant it. She never again even reached toward me when arriving or leaving. At first, I was relieved at her change in behavior, but as the years passed, I felt increasingly sad about what I had done in response to her kindness. But I couldn't figure out how to fix it. I thought of forcing myself to hug her, but I was afraid that, now that she had made her resolution never to touch me, that would be taken as a violation, or overstepping, on my part.

Whatever the origin of my shyness, it has stuck with me. Since I've been living in New York City, I haven't had any significant relationship with a woman. I do want contact with the opposite sex, but I don't know how to go about it. The idea of using an Internet dating service is too intimidating. And the normal course of my life—home, Subway, Subway, home—provides no social contact whatsoever.

This relationship with Niccole represented a new feature in my life, a change I was finding appealing.

4

"Where do your parents live?" Niccole and I were walking again in the park the following week. The weather had warmed considerably and the bright green leaves on the elms were starting to open. It was our third reinforcement exercise and the promised reward was a bouquet of white daffodils from Cliona's wagon.

"Are they well and everything?" Niccole continued.

"Yea, they're okay." I paused awkwardly. "They live in Florida, near Orlando. My dad took early retirement. He plays golf. Actually, we're not in touch that much."

"Do you have any brothers or sisters?" I realized that Niccole felt she was just making conversation, but she had hit a rather sensitive nerve.

"I'm afraid I'm an only child," I said. "Much to my parent's disappointment."

Niccole intuited that I didn't feel comfortable with the subject. "Look," she said, squeezing my arm, "there's a cardinal!" The big red bird was hopping on the grass just a few feet away. It pecked at the ground here and there with jerky motions, but I couldn't see that it was picking up anything to eat. It seemed like the pecking was a pointless nervous reflex.

"Hey," I said, "maybe you could use a bird book as a reward someday?"

"Good idea," she replied, squeezing my arm again. "If we're

going to explore nature," she said waving her arm at the park, "we should know what we're seeing! I read somewhere that New York City has over 200 species of birds. That seems ridiculously impossible." I filed the bird book idea away for future action.

"And what about your folks?" I asked.

My question triggered a silence. I turned and glanced at her face.

"I'm sorry," she said, looking away. "It's just a. . . difficult issue." After a pause she said, "My father died just a year ago."

"Oh, I'm sorry."

"It really was a shock for Mom and me. It was so sudden. A rare liver cancer. One day he was happily playing rummy with me on the deck, and the next he was in a hospital bed, for weeks and weeks. I remember, toward the end, him trying to talk to me. His lips were moving but no sound was coming out." Niccole's face tightened. I thought she might cry. "He was only 58, for goodness sakes."

"That is tough." I stopped and turned to sympathize with her. "Especially when it's sudden like that." Somehow, I felt it wouldn't be right to console her by hugging her, though that was probably what a person in this situation should do.

"I'm getting over it," she said, wiping her finger on her cheek, blinking hard. After a pause, she continued, "It's my mom I'm worried about. She's completely at a loss. It's like her life has lost all purpose. The house is a mess, and she used to be such a careful housekeeper. I go visit every few months, try to pick the place up. Last time I went, the sink was full of dirty dishes, there were corn flakes all over the kitchen floor. A layer of dust on everything, even on the phone by her bedside." She turned to me. "We get a lot of dust in Warren County, there's so many dirt roads."

"Where is that?" I asked.

"Western Pennsylvania. It's over 300 miles from here. Takes all day to get there."

We took a few more steps in silence along the concrete walkway, then Niccole continued. "Part of the problem is there's no one else. I'm an only child." She turned and gave me a significant nod. "Like you."

We walked quietly. "So she doesn't have anybody else to look after her. She sits all day in front of the TV—as bad as me with this stupid phone addiction. Maybe it runs in the genes?" she looked up at me, breaking into a smile.

"Mom needs to get into some activities. She does go to church, but that's about all." After a pause, she added, "I've really got to get back over there and check on her again. It's been two months since my last visit."

"Well," I said, "maybe she needs to get a job, a part-time job, or something?"

"Yes, something like that. I'm sure she'll get over it in the end," Niccole said, her cheerfulness returning. She tugged my hand. "Hey, I think I've achieved my goal again. It must be 30 minutes, right? Let's go back to Cliona."

* * *

Later that afternoon, back at the office, I thought about Niccole's question about my parents. She had brought up an awkward point. I generally don't like to talk much about my parents because there's quite a gap between us, both in distance and in communication. My father was a very successful real estate developer, with a combination of drive and people skills that enabled him to put together deals all around Bergen County, New Jersey (we lived in Englewood). His motto, which he repeated to me many times, especially when he found me doing something that seemed to him rather unproductive, was "Don't stroll through life, son. Stride!"

From a very early age, I understood that he wanted me to follow in his footsteps in the business world, but my personality wasn't suited to wheeling and dealing.

"Remember, you've got to look people in the eye," he would say to me, when criticizing me for not doing so. This advice never seemed to fit me. I have always found it rather disconcerting to stare at someone—and I don't like to be stared at. They say the eyes are the windows to the soul, and even from an early age, I've felt it impolite to intrude upon people's souls unless you know them really well.

I'd also been turned off by his emphasis on the importance of money. At the dinner table he would, well, brag, about deals he made and how many thousands of dollars of profit they brought him. Mother would nod appreciatively, but even as a child, I sensed there was something shallow about this focus. When he made these claims, I would look down at my plate. My father picked up on my indifferent attitude. "Don't underrate money, son! Money makes the world go round. That chicken leg you're eating comes from money."

It didn't help that I was an only child. In fact, I was a Caesarean birth—a difficult one that led my parents to decide not to try to have any more children. When I fully understood, in my teen years, how this birth meant that my mother couldn't have any more children, I began to see how this led my father to put even more pressure on me to succeed, to, as he kept putting it, "make something of myself."

Of course, he meant this in financial terms, but I had no interest in copying his career. He couldn't understand why I majored in English at Wesleyan. To his way of thinking, that was a field for school teachers. I tried to point out that this was my path to becoming a novelist, and that there's money to be made as an author.

"Karl Zimmerman earned four million last year," I told my father at one point. "For his novel *Primary Women*, about sex in the presidential election campaign. And it's been translated into 14 languages."

My father simply looked at the ceiling and smiled. I wasn't sure which idea he found so amusing, the topic of presidential sex or the idea of his child ever earning $4 million as an author.

When dad took early retirement, they moved to a swanky gated community in Florida near Orlando. Valencia Bay it's called. Out of obligation, I go visit them about once a year. It's a stressful few days, because we have little in common. Dad is an avid—and accomplished—golfer, but I have no interest in joining him in the sport. It doesn't appeal to me. It's too much like a performance on stage. When you're hitting the ball, everyone's watching—opponents, caddies, people in the clubhouse dining room. If you hit it into the trees, everyone politely looks away, but you know what they're thinking.

Actually, I have hit one world-famous golf shot, but not one that I can brag about. At my dad's insistence, I agreed to take a golf lesson when I made my first visit to Valencia Bay, just after

Mom and Dad moved there. Since I'm rather short (5'6") and light in weight, I don't really have a lot of meat to hit the ball very far even if I hit it correctly. Nick, the pro, was very patient with me, and fortunately the driving range was out behind the clubhouse where no one could observe my miscues. He took me through all the clubs, 9-iron, 8-iron, and so on, until finally we got to the one-wood, the driver. He was trying to show me how to drive the ball straight, but I scuffed. Even when I did hit the ball, it sliced off to the right.

"You're trying to swing too hard!" he kept saying.

Then, toward the end of the lesson, I hit a shot that I will never forget. My swing on this effort was much too low and the clubhead smashed into the dirt below the teed-up ball. It popped the ball straight up, 10 feet into the air right over my head. As it came down in front of me, I reached out with my right hand and caught it.

"Did I see what I just saw!?" said Nick, peering at me with amazement, hands on his hips. "Do you realize that you just caught your own drive?" He shook his head. "No pro in the history of golf has ever done that! And couldn't, even if he tried."

He gave me a big smile. "If golf had different rules, you'd be famous!"

Since they haven't changed the rules of golf, I keep this memorable tee shot to myself.

5

The air was mild that evening as we approached the Wagon Wheel Café on E. 46th Street. in the gathering darkness. There was little traffic on the street, just a few cabs. A number of people had grouped under the light outside the door, waiting for the Nanoelectronics support group to begin at 9 o'clock.

It had not been easy to persuade Niccole to come to this meeting. She's a very private person and found the idea of telling a group of strangers about herself quite daunting. I explained that she probably wouldn't have to say anything at all, that we could ask before it started if it would be all right for her not to talk. If they said she had to participate, she could decline to attend the group. Under these terms, she agreed to give it a try. Still, she was nervous about it, clinging tightly to my arm as we approached.

A tall woman holding a clipboard was standing with the group by the door. She checked her watch, then unlocked the door and pulled it open and everyone filed into the main dining area. As I learned later, the café closed for business at 3:00 p.m. The support group had a special arrangement with the owner who generously let them use a back room for their evening meeting. Once inside, the members moved to the inner room, making their way past the empty Formica tables with their neatly arranged menus and salt-and-pepper shakers. The woman with the clip-board stayed by the door of the inner room.

"Is this the support group for the phone people?" I asked.

"Yes, it is," she said with a cheerful smile. "Would you like to attend?"

"Well, Niccole here," I said, nodding, "is curious to see what goes on."

"Wonderful!" She addressed Niccole, reaching gently to touch her forearm. "We're so glad you're here! My name is Ginny."

Ginny had short brown hair and was wearing a full-length yellow skirt. I guessed she was about 40.

"We have one question," I said to her. "Does she have to participate? I mean, talk about herself?"

"Of course not. We're here to serve the members. Whatever they need." She paused. "When we start out, we do go around and invite everyone to give their first names. Would that be all right with you?"

Niccole gave an embarrassed smile. "I guess I can say my name out loud to 10 people."

I turned and looked carefully into her face. "So you want to try it?"

"Yes. . . yes." Niccole gave a tight nod and made a little laugh. "I'm sorry I'm making such a fuss."

Ginny reached out and put her hand on Niccole's shoulder. "That's fine, that's fine. We're so happy to have you. And by the way, if at any time you feel uncomfortable, we always say, people are free to leave."

Niccole paused at the door of the inner room. She turned back and gave me a worried glance. "I'll be here waiting for you, whenever you want," I said. I gave her a little wave with my fingertips.

Ginny closed the door on the group—which consisted of about a dozen people. Most of them were younger women, but there were at least three men and one older woman in a long green dress who appeared to be very sociable. I had seen her engaged in animated conversation with other members while they had been waiting outside the café.

Ginny had said the sessions lasted one hour, and that I was free to leave, but I felt I should wait in the main room of the café, in case Niccole needed to leave early. Just outside the door of the meeting room, on a chair, was a stack of papers. The members had each taken a copy as they filed into the room. I picked one up, seated myself in one of the booths and spread it before me on the tan plastic table.

I was surprised to see that it was handwritten in ink, but quite clear and readable. Then I noticed, at the bottom, those same letters I had seen before, "BHB." Again, I wondered what they stood for. I started to verbalize possibilities. Better Health. . . something? I racked my brains. Maybe, "Better Health and Beauty." It seemed like a good try, but it didn't allude to cell phones.

It was less than half a page, with the title, "Electronic Distractions and Time for Living."[1] I read it over several times. It certainly raised an important issue. I thought about my own life and had to admit that I hadn't had much in the way of social contact for years. Certainly, the idea of eating dinner with other people in their homes had gone out ages ago. And I didn't belong to a single volunteer group—hadn't been active in that way for years. In fact, as I thought about it, I hadn't been active as

---

[1]   The text of this document is included in the Appendix

a volunteer since my days at Wesleyan University when, in my junior and senior years, I was on the maintenance team for the disc golf course. That was nearly 10 years ago.

I lifted the page and gently fluttered it in front of me. I felt strangely divided about its message. I recognized that it made a valid point. But I also felt this piece of paper was judging me, and maybe it was being a bit unrealistic. After all, the world has changed and you can't fight change, right? Electronic technology is just a part of the world as it is. I neatly folded the document and slipped it in my jacket pocket, turning my thoughts to other things.

After an hour, the door to the meeting room opened and the members came out. They seemed relaxed and in good spirits, chatting and smiling. Niccole was very animated as she slipped up to me, eagerly grabbed my arm and looked into my face, her eyes bright. "It was really good," she said, nodding her head up and down.

Ginny came up and gave Niccole a sidewise hug. "She's an expert already," she said. Niccole looked pleased. I gathered she had participated in the discussion without any problem.

"By the way," I said, "I've been reading this." I tapped the paper in my hand. "Very interesting."

"Oh yes," said Ginny. "We had quite a discussion about it in there," she nodded toward the others. "We try to have a different topic of exploration each meeting to stimulate discussion."

As we turned to head out the door, Ginny said, looking at Niccole, "So, we'll see you in two weeks?"

"Oh yes," agreed Niccole enthusiastically. "By the way, is there something I can bring?" The group had shared oatmeal cookies and cider during the meeting.

"Don't you worry about it, dear," Ginny said with a little laugh. "One privilege of being a newcomer is that you get free food." We all smiled.

"So we're coming back in two weeks?" I asked as we walked up the nearly deserted street, heading to the Subway station on 6th Avenue.

"Oh yes, definitely!" said Niccole, squeezing my arm, glancing into my face with a bright smile. "They were very interesting people. Ginny is very good at directing the discussion. And Rebecca is so sweet! And then there is George, the one wearing the bright yellow T-shirt." She stopped walking and turned to me. "You know, he threw his phone off the George Washington Bridge!"

"What!?"

"Yes. Into the Hudson River. He went on the pedestrian walkway exactly to the middle, to the sign that marks the border between New York State and New Jersey. He made a big ritual out of it, even read a poem by somebody—I don't remember the name—out loud. He said it was the high point of his life; that it changed everything. This was about two years ago. Actually, George is not even his real name. It's a new nickname—after the bridge thing. One of the members called him that in fun, and it seemed right. He felt that leaving behind his old name was a kind of rebirth, he said. He's happy to be called George."

"So maybe we should go up there to the bridge tonight?" I asked with a grin, tugging her waist against mine. "Then I could call you Georgette."

"Oh no, no." Niccole shook her head, laughing at first, but then getting serious. "Everybody said that it's very important to prepare long and carefully for any major change in phone use. Because it's become such a deep part of your life. George gave it a year, between deciding to get rid of the phone and actually doing it. He said that when the time came, he was more than ready."

I was happy to see that this support group was such a positive experience for Niccole. She had told them about our 30-minute exercise in the park—obviously, her fears of speaking in public had abated—and group members had said it was an excellent tactic and should be repeated.

"By the way," I said, taking the copy of the discussion paper from my pocket, "do you know what 'BHB' stands for?"

She peered at the piece of paper. "No, it never came up. I assumed it's the initials of the person who wrote it."

"I doubt that," I said. "I've seen these letters before on other documents. It's a bit mysterious. I've tried to look them up, but there's nothing on the Internet about it. Seems to be some kind of organization that doesn't want people to know it exists." We continued walking in silence under streetlights.

"It seems," I said, thinking out loud, "like something an investigative reporter ought to look into."

6

On the following Monday, going through the pile of mail and circulars on the table in the hall, I discovered a letter from Davidson and Small, the literary agency where Steve Small was considering *Prisoner of Love*. I gave a little gasp. What, I wondered, did Small's use of the physical mail service, instead of a phone call or e-mail, portend? One possibility was that a physical document was being used because it was a very official, contractual 'yes.' On the other hand, it could be that it was a 'no,' that Steve was using a letter to let me down carefully and politely.

I twisted the smooth tan envelope in my fingers, looking at the ceiling for a long moment. Finally, I went to my desk and rummaged in the top drawer for the brass letter opener I use for checks and other important documents. I carefully sliced the envelope open and let the neatly-folded page drop to the desk. Almost as soon as I unfolded it, I saw that the answer was no. My eye fell on Steve's polite words, "You have great talent as a writer . . . I'm sure you'll go far," and so on. But the answer was still no: "unable to pursue this opportunity further at the present time."

In explanation, he said that "science fiction is a weak market once you go outside the hack themes of zombies, space invaders and planetary travel. Time travel did well when H. G. Wells started it, but it's getting old now." He also added a quasi-compliment, saying, "Your strength as a writer is not so much in the development of character, which is the basis of fiction, but in the analysis of ideas. You should think about doing non-fiction, things like politics, social themes, or current history. You have some real talent there." He signed off stating, "Keep in touch."

I gave a long exhale. My shoulders slumped. Two years of writing and re-writing: all down the drain!

When I went out to meet Niccole in the park for our session at 11:00 a.m., the disappointment was still weighing on my mind, and it must have shown.

"Is anything the matter?" she asked. "You look kind of serious."

"It's a long story," I said, looking up at the sky before beginning my answer.

"Remember that book I told you I was working on, the time-traveling romance novel?" She nodded.

"Well, it's been rejected."

She gave me a look of intense sympathy. "But surely you can submit it to someone else?"

I sighed. "Well, I could. But I don't think it has much chance. Apparently, the whole genre is wrong. The market for time travel just isn't there. At least, that's what the agent said. Here's his letter." I handed her the document that I had been carrying in my back pocket.

She unfolded it and studied it carefully, frowning. Then her face brightened. "He says you have talent for something about public affairs, social issues. You can do that! In fact, he's practically committed himself to accepting a book of that kind."

I saw that she did have a point. In trying to let me down gently, Steve had committed himself to at least looking at an MS of mine in the non-fiction genre. That opened a new possibility.

To become a successful author, you didn't have to write a novel of fiction, as I had been assuming. There were plenty of famous authors writing exposés and reports on social topics. But what should it be? Well, I thought, there's a whole world out there of wrongs and injustices. I'll just have to keep my eyes open.

"Good idea. Good idea," I said, nodding slowly.

I straightened and looked at her smile. "Well, anyway," I said stuffing the letter back in my pocket, "it's time to pick out some flowers and do our reinforcement session."

The walk around the park was rather quiet, as both of us were in a subdued mood. At one point, Niccole grabbed my hand and gave it a sympathetic squeeze. I smiled in appreciation of her concern.

At the end of our walkaround and after the flower reward at Cliona's cart, Niccole turned to me as we were parting at the curb. "You need some R&R. Really!" She looked firmly into my eyes. "I would like to invite you to dinner. Friday night, at the Shamrock Grill. Will that work?"

Her frank proposal took me by surprise. "Well, uh, that's. . . that's very kind of you. Sure, yes, let's. . ." I nodded vigorously.

"It's time for *me* to be the therapist," she said, smiling brightly and squeezing my hand again.

Back at the office, I reflected on the morning's accomplishment. I was going on a date! In point of fact, it was my first actual date in years.

Ironies of ironies, it exactly duplicated the first date of my high school years, with Nancy Dawson. It was the Sadie Hawkins dance, where the girls are supposed to ask the boys, and she had asked me. That really was a funny idea, the Sadie Hawkins dance.

It wasn't until many years later that I found out where the custom came from—and it isn't very flattering for women. It's based on a cartoon series by Al Capp about Kentucky hillbillies. Sadie Hawkins is a young woman so unattractive that no one wants to marry her. In fact, she is the ugliest girl in town. Capp drew her face with separated buck teeth, and a large crooked nose. To keep her from becoming a spinster—apparently the worst thing that can happen to a woman in that subculture—her wealthy, powerful father invents a footrace where Sadie chases men and the man she catches is forced to marry her. As the story turns out, Sadie catches the most handsome boy in town.

This, I thought, has been my Sadie Hawkins Day, only it was the prettiest girl in town chasing me!

The Shamrock Grill, on 63rd Street, where we met that Friday evening, is an ancient establishment. I've heard it dates back to the 1920s, and it certainly looks like it, with its ornately-designed white tin ceiling and dark oak molding running high up the walls. You almost expect an Irish leprechaun to come dancing out of the kitchen waving a shamrock. The place was quite crowded. We had to wait 20 minutes to be seated, enjoying the heady odor of Guinness and frying food.

Naturally, I was curious about Niccole's background. While we were waiting for a table, I started my exploration cautiously, asking simple questions about where she was born and so on. She had grown up in rural Pennsylvania, about 60 miles north of Pittsburgh, where her mother still lived. After high school, she had gone on to Alfred University, where she majored in art. I hadn't even heard of this little college, located in rural New York State, further west than Cornell at Ithaca. Even though she had lived in New York City for the past six years, she was not comfortable with city life, with its density of people and buildings. She was a small-town girl at heart.

The waiter had just cleared the dinner plates and we were waiting for coffee when I edged into a question about her previous relationships.

"Do you have a very active social life? I mean, I gather you haven't been married, right?" Niccole looked up and gave me a guarded smile, but she didn't answer at first.

After a few moments, she said in a rather serious tone, "I haven't been within 50 miles of marriage." She gave a little laugh.

I was at a bit of a loss about how to continue. I decided to try a little humor. "Is that because you hate men?"

She smiled at my wisecrack, then, speaking seriously, said, "That's a good question." After a pause, she reached and put her hand over mine. "Of course, I don't hate men," she said with energy. "I get along fine with men," she said. "Some men," she added with a wink.

"Hate isn't the word for it," she continued thoughtfully, looking at the table. "But there is something. Actually, it's a kind of. . . well, anxiousness."

"You're afraid of something. . . ?"

"Well, you could say that." After a pause she said, "I guess this started in high school. The boys seemed so pushy. It was like there was a contest going on over who is making out with whom." She looked down. "Making out," she continued, speaking more to herself than to me. "What did that mean? Holding hands? Hugging? Kissing? I was never very clear about it. It was like some kind of contest. I just didn't want to have anything to do with it."

She looked down. Her words touched on my own awkwardness about the dating situation.

"That. . . that seems to be my pattern with men," Niccole continued, looking up at me. "They're too aggressive. They seem to always want to grab you. I guess some other girls like it, but it really turns me off. I sometimes think I was born in the wrong century. I would do better in the olden days when men wore high hats, stayed 9 feet away and bowed politely."

I didn't know what to say.

"Don't get me wrong. I can be attracted to men, but it's just that they move so fast, they're so aggressive." After a pause, she looked up, into my eyes. "You're different. You're not aggressive. You're sort of polite, actually. Like a 19th-century gentleman." That made me grin.

"I mean it," she said, pressing her hand on mine. "I couldn't imagine you ever attacking anybody."

"Well, you're right about that," I said, quite seriously. "Actually, I've been shy about approaching women, physically, that is."

"I could tell that," Niccole said, "from our first meeting. That you wanted to hang back." After a pause, she said, "I've never told anyone else all this about my high school days."

"Well. . . well," I stammered. "I suppose that's a good thing? I mean that you finally spoke about it. Isn't it?"

She playfully tugged my sleeve. "Of course, it is! Stop being so worried about things!" We looked into each other's eyes, smiling.

Then she asked, "I don't suppose you've been married very many times, either?" I laughed at her allusion to my first question.

"No, no," I shook my head. "Actually, I haven't even been close. I didn't have a first date until I was a sophomore in high school. It's a little embarrassing to have to admit." I gave a little shrug. "Nancy Dawson. A very quiet, polite girl. She wore a long blue dress that covered her ankles. I remember sitting with her at the side of the dance floor, it was in the gym—the Sadie Hawkins Dance—trying to think of something to talk about. I asked her which teacher she liked, and then we got to talking about Mrs. Driscoll, the social studies teacher who made the worst boy troublemakers sit in front. That was years and years ago but that's what I remember about my first date. Talking about the stern Mrs. Driscoll. So. . ." I shrugged and smiled, "Not a profoundly romantic encounter."

Niccole and I were silent for a moment. "And another thing," I said, "is that lately, I don't seem to meet anyone. In fact," I said, nodding gently at her, "this is the first actual date I've had for years. I'm just not in contact with women in my daily life. I don't want to use the dating sites. So much pretentiousness and deception—the whole idea turns me off."

"Me, too," said Niccole. "I would never know what I was getting myself in for."

"And without those," I continued, "you don't seem to meet people anymore. All the usual places where people used to connect—clubs, hobbies, sports—have pretty much gone away."

"There's only work," Niccole said, "and even there you are not actually working alongside people. I have three co-workers, in addition to my boss. Even though they're just a few feet away in their offices down the hall, I see them very little. We're mostly just texting each other. The other day I complimented Jason, the bookkeeper, on getting rid of his beard. He said he had shaved it off two weeks ago, but that was the first time I'd actually seen his face. So, you're right, there's not much direct contact."

I smiled at her and said, "So, unless you were to look out your window and see someone on a park bench using her phone. . .?"

Niccole gave a broad smile. "Exactly!"

7

"Well, what shall we use as a reward instead?" I asked.

It was Thursday, and Niccole and I were aiming for another session in Thompkins Square, visiting with Cliona and walking around phone-less for 30 minutes. It was becoming clear to both of us that our sessions were becoming more than a simple therapeutic exercise, a point that became dramatically obvious on this day when Cliona didn't happen to be there with her flowers.

In answer to my question, Niccole gave a knowing, secretive smile.

"Yes? What is it?" I prodded.

She looked from side to side, giggling. Still, she didn't speak, but looked into my eyes with a penetrating stare.

"Yes?" I wondered what she had in mind.

Finally, she spoke. "Well, one possibility would be. . . a kiss." She quickly added, "It could be on the cheek." After a little pause she winked. "It would be a lot cheaper than flowers." Then her look became serious, "I mean, if you don't mind."

"Well," I said drawing the word out slowly. I suppose most men would have leaped at this invitation to kiss a beautiful woman, but for me it felt rather awkward. Don't get me wrong: I want this contact. In fact, I fantasize about it, a lot. But in the real world, as I had told Niccole the other night at the Shamrock Grill, with a flesh and blood woman, at first there's a shyness.

I wasn't sure, but it seemed she was opening the door to a kiss on the lips. I still remember my first kiss, which took place when I was a senior in high school. A senior, mind you. That's how 'slow' I was to get intimate with the girls I dated. It was toward the end of the school year and Sue Noll and I had gone out to Crispin Lake on a nice, warm sunny day to sunbathe. I really liked Sue a lot. She had short blond hair that set off her cheerful smile, and had a very patient, sensitive spirit. In some ways, she seemed years older than me in wisdom and maturity. Almost like a mother.

Her father was the manager of A-1 Foods and they lived in Glenwood Park. After the Tristan Merkel concert, I held her hand while walking her home, which had become a regular custom after our dates, but that was as far as I had the courage to go.

Then, there on the beach in Crispin Park, it happened. We were lying on our backs enjoying the Spring sunshine looking at the sky—the water was too cold to think about swimming—Sue rose up beside me and leaned over me, bringing her face closer and closer to mine, but holding back from actually kissing me. Finally, when her lips were about 3/32th of an inch away from mine, I felt compelled to end the awkward situation, and raised my head ever so slightly and pressed my lips against hers. So, technically, *I* kissed *her*, although the fact of the matter was that she did 95% of the work in making it happen. Of course, I was thrilled.

Since that time, I have become somewhat more comfortable about making physical contact with a woman. I can hold hands without much problem, even on a first date. But there's still plenty of awkwardness when it comes to physical contact with someone I'm just getting to know. That's why I hesitated when Niccole suggested the kiss as a reward. Of course, I realized that in making the proposition, Niccole was opening herself up to me with great frankness.

"I. . . I think. . . that is a very clever idea," I said. "It's. . . It's kind of original, really." I swallowed. "Now, I may not be so good at it, because I can be shy at first, like I've told you, but if you'll be patient, I think it will work very well."

Niccole broke out in a big, knowing smile and positively jammed her phone into my hand.

There was an air of excitement between us as we started our walk around the park. Niccole worked extra hard making conversation to help cover up my uneasiness. She talked a lot about her job at the Everett Company, where she had been working for five years—she's 27, by the way. She appreciated the steady employment but felt it had become quite limiting. It had been over a year since she had been asked to make any kind of floral or natural design for a piece of furniture. All she did now was lay out measurements, specify colors, and research the availability of raw materials. "It's really time for me to move on, if I had the courage to start something new." As I pointed out to her, I was in exactly the same place with my job at Ringo.

When my watch showed that the time had come to declare the phone deprivation exercise complete, we stopped walking and faced each other. Of course, I was willing to kiss her, but I felt awkward.

I carefully reached around her shoulder. "I may not be so good at this," I said, half smiling, half serious. "But," I continued, looking her in the eyes, "I want you to know my heart is in the right place."

Well, there was no shyness on her part! She put her arms around my neck and pulled my face closer and closer to hers. When my lips were but a fraction of an inch from hers, I did the last bit and pushed my lips onto hers. So, with this kissing business, history sort of repeated itself.

* * *

As the weeks passed, the kiss with Niccole in the park, and our conversation about neither of us being married, opened my thinking to a topic that had lain quite out of sight for me for quite some time. In fact, I hadn't thought seriously about the subject of marriage since those high school senior days with Sue Noll. I had gotten pretty involved with Sue after our little tryst at Crispin Lake, necking a lot, as a matter of fact. But we were headed in different directions, me to Wesleyan and she to, of all places, the University of Virginia—her brother was already attending there. This put us many miles apart. We could only write letters and make phone calls, which got less and less frequent as time went by.

I guess it's true that the weakening of the relationship was mainly my fault. I just wasn't ready, at age 18, to sign up for a total life commitment. Sue was. I knew, from the way she talked about it, that her main focus in life was getting married and having a family. She didn't quite say so, but she let me understand that if I wasn't going to step up, she would find somebody else. And she did. In her junior year she sent me the famous Dear John letter—

Dear Jon, in my case—explaining that she had gotten (as she put it) "close to someone who is becoming very important in my life." So that was that. I didn't feel any sense of anger or loss. In fact, I think I was relieved. From my perspective, there was a whole wide world out there, and now I had it all to explore.

Now, with Niccole getting rather close—and rather intimate—the marriage possibility presented itself for the second time in my life. There was an openness and frankness about her that made her special. Unlike other women friends I have had, Niccole wasn't guarded or artificial about her real feelings. If she didn't like your haircut, or the way you poked her ribs, she was frank and open about it—and if she *did* like it, she also said so. I found I missed being away from her, and looked forward to seeing her each time we got back together.

But marriage? In my eight years in New York, I've become very self-sufficient—and self-oriented. I make my own suppers. I clean the apartment—well, sort of, when it really needs it. There are plenty of movies to watch. And to break the monotony, I go on my yearly expeditions, gathering material for my writing.

On my visit to Orlando this past December, my dad teased me about becoming a "confirmed bachelor," urging me to "see more women." Mother didn't say anything—she's more sensitive about my feelings—but I could see from the gentle smile on her face that she endorsed his advice. Of course, I understand. They want to become grandparents, and, as their only child, this ambition rests entirely with me.

I thought about the point on my flight back to New York. Is there anything wrong with being a confirmed bachelor? Is everyone required to get married and settle down in Englewood, have children to raise, and a lawn to mow every Saturday? This didn't seem like the life for me. It certainly isn't the life of a writer. Hemingway, Dos Passos, F. Scott Fitzgerald, and the rest: they were free spirits. Yes, maybe they weren't so socially well-adjusted as they should have been, but almost by definition, famous writers aren't happily married suburbanites. As I watched the tiny highways below the plane stretching in their distant directions, this feeling deepened, this sense that being free and independent was the best fit for me.

Now this seemingly sensible conclusion was starting to be challenged, or at least questioned, by the growing closeness with Niccole.

8

At the next meeting of the phone support group, while the members were gathering in the Wagon Wheel Café, I got a chance to ask Ginny about the puzzling acronym, BHB. There was another handout sheet on the chair which I had picked up and studied. It was a different text—typed-out this time—but, sure enough, it had those same initials at the bottom.

Holding it in my hand, pointing at the letters, I asked her, with intense curiosity in my voice, "What do these letters, B.H.B., mean?"

"Being human being—you didn't know that?" Ginny looked surprised. "Heavens, it's what everyone's doing these days. Rebecca is an organizer." She called over to the older woman who was wearing the same green dress as last week. "Rebecca, this gentleman wants to know about BHB."

Rebecca made her way around the others to me.

"Yes, I'm curious about this group," I said, pointing at the letters at the bottom of the page. "What does it do?"

Rebecca gave a broad smile but seemed hesitant to begin speaking.

"My name's Jon, by the way," I said, and stuck out my hand. "I'm with Niccole."

"Yes, of course. It's a pleasure to meet you, Jon," she said, taking my hand. "And we just love Niccole! She such a wonderful

56

addition to our group." After a pause, she said, going back to my original question, "Well, it's a little complicated." She paused. "You might say we are discussion groups—but also action groups."

"And what is your purpose?"

She paused. "Well, I joined because I'm interested in helping people. We figure out ways to help them lead more creative lives."

"That sounds like a good idea," I said. "But what about technology? I thought that the aim was opposing electronic things and technology? Like this group opposes phones, right?"

"Well, yes, to some extent," she said. There was hesitation in her tone. "To tell you the truth, I'm not very expert on that side of it, but"—she looked over to the door of the meeting room where Ginny was waving—"we have to start the group now. We'll talk more after." She gave me a warm smile and went in with Ginny. The door closed behind them.

I took my seat at the Formica table in the booth in the empty dining room and examined the handout sheet. The title was "The Power of Boredom."[2] It couldn't have been more than 150 words. I read it through several times, and I guess I could see the point. Like everyone else, I have tended to assume that any new technology is an advance. Phonographs, electric lights, radio, television, computers, rocket ships—these are achievements. They make life better. They advance the human race.

But maybe, as this document suggested, there was a down side—at least sometimes. The thought brought to mind an episode of my boyhood. For years we had a push mower and it was my job, each Saturday, to mow the lawn with it. Then Dad got

---

a power mower, one of the new rotaries, with a gas engine and big blades that create a cyclone of destruction underneath. Well one day—I guess I wasn't paying attention, thinking of something else—I ran over Mom's little kneeling pad she had left on the lawn beside the front garden. The blades blasted it to pieces and sprayed out a cloud of white Styrofoam bits! For weeks afterward, she gave me looks of censure.

I remember how she also used to complain about the noise of the mower. She said it sounded like an airplane trying to take off and never succeeding. Thinking about it while sitting there at the table that evening in the Wagon Wheel, I did feel that maybe the gas mower wasn't all that great, that there was something healthier, and saner, about the old push mower.

In due course, the support group finished and the members streamed out of the room. Rebecca was among the first and she headed to me.

"I am sorry our conversation was interrupted," she said. "You were asking about BHB and I decided the best way to answer would be to read this." She lifted a piece of paper she had in her hand and read its words out to me, slowly and carefully: "We are seeking to elicit the positive human qualities that are often compromised by technological evolution." Smiling, she looked up and gave a firm nod. "There. Now you know."

I didn't quite know how to respond, for you can't exactly argue with a piece of paper.

When I didn't say anything, Rebecca continued, "I know I shouldn't have to read it, but I'm just not good at explaining things. When people used to ask me about what BHB is, I would get bogged down in a long discussion, and always come away feeling that I hadn't really answered their question. So that's why I use this," she said, waving the paper.

"And where did you get that?" I said indicating the paper. "Is that a publication of the BHB organization?"

Rebecca looked puzzled. "I don't know anything about that. I copied it down from a prompt we had in an exploration a while ago. I realized it put the idea in a nutshell. Look," she continued, "if you're interested in finding out more, we'd love to have you at our exploration. It meets every other week."

"Well," I said, a little surprised at the suddenness of the invitation, "I do think I would like to find out more. It just seems so. . .so different. How many of these groups are there?"

"Oh, there must be 30 or 40 in Manhattan."

"And why haven't I heard about them?" I asked. "Do they have a national organization? Or a website I can go to?"

"No, actually, they don't."

"Why not?"

She paused. "It's complicated." She gave another big smile. "I'm sorry, I keep saying that, don't I?" After a little pause, she said, "Let's just say we're a little shy about publicity."

"Wow!" I said. "It sounds sort of like a. . . secret group?" She continued smiling but didn't say anything. I went on, "So you really are anti-technology?"

"There's more to it than that." Again, a pause. It was starting to seem like this conversation was more pauses than words.

She raised her open palms. "After all, if you step under a tree to get out of the rain, you could say that's technology, right?"

I frowned at what seemed an odd illustration.

"You're using a physical apparatus to gratify your desires.

That's the example Victor uses—he's one of our members. Anyway, the point is to think about technology, to weigh it, not just lap it up." She smiled at my puzzled look. "But we can go into all that at the meeting." She reached out and gently touched my elbow. "We'd love to have you join us."

I took down the meeting time, which was on the following Tuesday. The address was at 186th Street in Washington Heights, a little far from my apartment on E. 47th Street, but my curiosity was aroused. I told her I would like to attend.

That evening, as I sat at my desk making a note of the BHB meeting on my calendar, it occurred to me that, in addition to satisfying my curiosity, observing this unusual gathering was a professional opportunity for me as a writer. This relatively unknown organization could be the basis for a story for the *Times* or somebody. After all, everyone has been talking for years about how technology is taking control of our lives, causing all kinds of bad side effects. If this unknown, anti-technology movement really did have hundreds, or even thousands, of members, it would be significant news.

In fact, maybe not just an article. The idea hit me like a glowing sunrise: Maybe exposing this secret anti-technology organization could be a best-selling book! A non-fiction book of the kind that Steve Small, my (let's hope!) agent, thinks I would be good at—and which he would be willing to seriously consider.

I tapped my pencil point on the blotter, faster and faster. Yes, this could really put my career as a writer back on track!

9

At our next meeting in the park, I was mistaken for a male abuser.

The confusion grew out of my idea of trying out a different technique for drawing Niccole away from her attachment to her phone. I was a little anxious about it because it seemed a bit intrusive—and also rather advanced as a clinical technique. Perhaps not something for an untrained amateur to administer. Niccole shared none of this hesitation, however, and smiled brightly as I tried to explain it.

"It's called 'distractive therapy.' I read about it online. With the positive reinforcement therapy that we've been using, you get a reward"—we grinned at each other, knowing, of course, that this reward had become our kissing (which, by the way, was getting extremely natural)—"for avoiding the undesired, habitual behavior. With distractive therapy. . . ."

Niccole looked up at me with expectation written all across her face. Her eagerness made me a little nervous. It seemed that I was rather stepping into the role of doctor, becoming responsible for curing her.

"Well anyway," I continued, "the way it works is you get busy doing something you like, and then you have to put it away in order to engage in the bad habit."

A puzzled look crossed her face.

"So the result is that you come to see the habit as unpleasant, unappealing." She nodded, though I could see she was still uncertain.

"What I have in mind," I continued, "is, we get you an ice cream cup from over there"—I pointed to the Good Humor truck parked on the street—"and you start to eat it. Then, at various points, I tell you to stop, and you have to use your phone. In this way it trains you to feel that the phone is a negative experience, because it takes you away from a positive experience. Got it?"

Her puzzled expression melted into an indulgent smile. I could tell she still didn't entirely understand, but she was willing to try whatever I had in mind.

"Just wait here." I stood up. "What's your favorite ice cream?"

"Strawberry."

I went to the truck and bought a cup of strawberry ice cream from the young man.

Back at the bench, I tore the lid off and put the cup in her hand, then gave her the little wooden spoon.

"Now you're to eat this, but whenever I say 'STOP,' you have to immediately put it down, take up your phone and play that solitaire inversion game. Got it?"

Niccole was holding her lips closed, repressing laughter. She gave a little nod.

"Eat!" I said.

She continued grinning at me. "Eat, eat," I said, urging her with my hand. She gave a gentle shrug, turned to the ice cream and began to dig a little portion of the pink sweetness from the hard surface. I let her enjoy the first spoonful. Then, just as she was about to put the second spoonful in her mouth, I said, "STOP!"

She put the spoon down and looked at me.

"Take the phone," I said, pointing at it. "Start using it."

She set the ice cream dish aside on the bench and took the phone and began touching at the screen. After 20 seconds, I said, "Okay, put it down and go back to the ice cream." She did as I directed.

As we were engaged in this process, with me repeatedly barking my "STOP" command and Niccole quietly obeying, I noticed out of the corner of my eye that we were being observed by a man who had been approaching along the walk. He was an older man with silver-gray hair, wearing a dark blue suit. He looked like a banker. He had paused on the sidewalk and was inspecting us ever more carefully. He seemed concerned.

I had just given another of my firm "STOP" commands. He walked quickly up to us.

"Is everything all right?" he asked, addressing Niccole. "I mean, if he's harming you. . . ?"

Niccole giggled. "Oh no, it's fine," she said.

"Well, if you need help. . ." he said to her. He glanced at me suspiciously. "He is ordering you. . . ?"

"No, no we're fine. Really," Niccole said again, grinning.

The man was obviously perplexed about what we had been doing, still not convinced it was harmless. And I couldn't say that I blamed him, because from a distance it could look like some kind of abuse was going on. I tried to explain.

"This is a technique for training someone to be less dependent on their smartphone," I said, and went on to describe the distractive therapy idea.

"Oh, well, that really does account for it," he said. "And now

I've got to explain my own behavior, which, I now see, you could consider rather rude. After all, it really was none of my business. I really have to apologize." After a pause he went on, "Actually, I was trying to carry out an idea that I'm supposed to apply.

"You see, I've joined a group of people who. . ." he paused, apparently finding it difficult to put in words. "Well, anyway, we want to be concerned about other people, to personally add to their lives. We each have a little assignment, every month, of looking for a way to assist a stranger. We call it a 'spark.' So, this was supposed to be my helping act. Obviously, I really goofed." He bowed his head. "I'm so sorry."

"No problem," I said.

"Well, that's kind of you to forgive me," he said turning to go. At that moment a thought struck me.

"By the way," I said, "what's the name of your group."

He turned his head back toward us as he walked away, "We call ourselves BHB."

Since he was leaving, it didn't seem appropriate to call him back to elaborate on this remarkable declaration.

"Is that the same BHB you were asking Ginny about?" asked Niccole.

"I don't know," I said, staring thoughtfully at the man in the distance. "If it is, there's even more of a story here than I thought."

Niccole was still holding the ice cream cup. I returned to the project at hand.

"Well, I guess we have finished this experiment. Eat up and enjoy."

She did so—slipping a dab of the ice cream between my lips in between her portions. When we had finished the cup, I asked,

"So, any reactions, one way or the other?"

Niccole smiled knowingly at me. "The ice cream was very good," she teased.

"You know what I mean. Seriously?"

She stared thoughtfully along the brick walkway for a moment. She looked up, smiling broadly. "If you really want to know, this may not be the kind of conditioning you had in mind."

"What do you mean?"

She paused. "I'm enjoying being with you and the phone is the cause of that. That's what's bringing us together. Don't you see that?"

When I didn't say anything, she went on. "So the theory I'm apparently being taught is, in order to keep you"—she nodded at me—"I have to keep this," she said, playfully caressing her cheek with the phone. Her eyes were dancing. I knew she was teasing, but she did have a point. The reinforcement theory was getting somewhat off the rails.

"No, no, no!" I said energetically. "Yes, of course this is all fun. But we can get along together without the phone." I paused. "You'll see. When we have the day that I'm planning, the day without the phone."

She lit up. Her smile was so bright I almost needed sunglasses to look at it.

10

It was good I gave myself a full hour to make it to 186th Street. The Local unit on the Eighth Ave. Subway line, which I had transferred to at 145th Street didn't arrive to pick me up for over 15 minutes. It really would be gauche, I thought, as the car clicked and swayed up the tunnel, to arrive late to my first meeting of a BHB. In the end, it was 7:55 p.m. when I arrived at the address Rebecca had given me. As I hurriedly finished the flight of stairs and exited the stairwell, I saw the door to apartment 3P was open. Rebecca was standing near the entrance and she greeted me.

"You made it! I'm so glad you could come," she said brightly. "Here we all are." She gestured toward the rest of the group. She pointed to a young man in a red shirt standing by the door. "This is Niko. This is his apartment, which he graciously allows us to use."

I reached out and shook his hand.

On entering the room, I noticed colorful fabrics hanging on the walls, vivid purples and reds, which seemed like Tibetan prayer shawls. Dangling from the light fixture in the center of the ceiling was a shiny little brass half-moon. There were about 10 people in the room, both men and women, mostly young. Rebecca was probably the oldest of the group.

I was impressed by the animation of the conversation among the members. They were using their hands energetically, nodding vigorously as they made points and reacted to the ideas of others.

Rebecca announced my presence to the group. "This is Jon Jones. He's come all the way from East 47th Street to find out about BHB." The members looked over, nodding with interest. Several gave little hello hand waves.

"How long did it take you on the Subway?" asked a young man on my left. He was wearing a yellow T-shirt that had writing in dark blue letters, **Contents: 1 Human (may contain gluten)**. The humor of it distracted me for a second.

"This is Malcolm," said Rebecca, gesturing toward him. "He's one of the founders of this circle." Malcolm smiled.

"Good to meet you," I said, nodding. "About an hour. There was a delay with the Local."

"There's technology for you," said a young woman in a bright purple dress seated on the far side of the circle. There was a humorous tone in her voice. Several others chuckled knowingly.

Rebecca smiled, then explained, "We are all from this neighborhood, so we walked here. I'm sure, if you decide you're interested in BHB, we can find a circle for you that meets near East 47th Street. Now"—she continued, handing me a sheet of paper—"this is today's prompt. The other members got it last meeting, so they've been able to think about it for several weeks. Maybe you'll get a chance to skim it."

I sat down on the folding chair next to Rebecca. I took a quick look at the page and saw the title, which was "Humility."[3] It was very short, hardly more than a paragraph, nothing like the lengthy literary disquisition one might expect. I noticed the letters BHB

---

[3] The text of this document is included in the Appendix.

stood at the bottom. The first sentence said something about monkeys, but I had no time to read further.

"Ted, why don't you begin," said Rebecca.

"Well," said a young man with a well-developed, fluffy brown beard who was wearing a loose, white muslin shirt, "I could be wrong, but. . . ."

Everyone around the circle laughed heartily. I gathered it was some kind of inside joke.

"No, I think it's a good point," Ted continued. "If we could recognize that any belief we have is tentative." He opened his hands. "I mean: Imagine what the world would have been spared if Hitler had had some humility. If he had considered that he could be wrong. That's the problem with politics. Everyone's so certain about things." Other members of the group were nodding their heads.

The young woman in blue tights on my left was especially vigorous in her affirmation. "Ted's right. Like, take the President. He's been in the White House for two years. Has he ever started a speech with, 'I could be wrong, but'?" The others nodded in amusement. "It seems that in politics," she went on, "everyone feels they have to pound the table. There's no spirit of humility." Then she added, smiling broadly, "But I could be wrong." The others smiled knowingly.

"Well, isn't that what comes from massification?" Ted said.

I was starting to feel quite lost with this new phraseology. I wondered if there might be a glossary or a pamphlet that this organization put out that defined these terms.

Ted was continuing his point: "They're trying to communicate with large numbers of people at the same time. To appeal to the mob, you have to project certainty." He smiled. "I mean, would you expect the leader of a revolution to say, 'We demand justice, but I could be wrong'?" The group laughed again. "But I'm preaching to the choir," he said, looking around at the group with a little smile.

As the discussion proceeded, I noticed an unusual thing— or rather, the unusual absence of something: nobody took out a phone or any other device, not even to sneak a quick look at it. At a meeting of this many people, that seemed very unusual. Also, so far as I could tell from checking hip pockets and shirt pockets, no one had a phone. It made me feel a little guilty about mine in the pocket of my blazer. Of course, I had turned it off.

After some more discussion about politics, an older man with black-framed glasses spoke. "What about the monkey analogy? I find that a little offensive. Aren't we smarter than monkeys?" What do you think, Louise?" he said, addressing the young woman on his left.

"Was Hitler smarter than a monkey?" Her tone was serious. "His emotionalism brought ruin to millions of his own people— and to himself!" Many nodded thoughtfully.

The comments on this and related topics continued for about half an hour. I was intrigued, but only half-able to grasp the points. I felt more confused about the BHB business than ever. I couldn't make out its purpose. This group certainly didn't seem like a political action group.

After some time, Rebecca brought the discussion to a halt, saying, "Well, we'll just have to keep wrestling with this, won't we?"

She smiled at the group, and continued, "Now it's time for springs and sparks. Anybody want to begin?"

I had no idea what those words meant, of course. Even after people began talking, the subject still wasn't clear to me.

The woman in the purple dress began. Smiling broadly, she addressed the group, "Well, I finally did it!"

Everyone looked at her with interest. The man sitting next to her asked, "You mean, the Toyota?"

"Yes!" she said, grinning broadly. She thrust her fist into the air in a gesture of victory. Others murmured expressions of praise.

Rebecca leaned toward me and said quietly, nodding at the woman, "That's Lindsey. She's been aiming at doing without her car." I still didn't quite understand.

"Was it hard?" the man asked.

"No, not at all," Lindsey replied. "When I have to go to New Haven, I take the train—which takes a little longer than before. But I get to meet people on the train. And doing without the car forces me to do more shopping at the neighborhood stores. So, I'm shopping smaller," she said with a proud grin.

"Here, here!" said one of the younger men. I gathered from this that the group was opposed to 'big box' stores, and probably resisted Internet shopping, as well.

"Of course, it means more walking," Lindsey continued. "But that's good for me too, right?" She glanced around the room. "Last Saturday, I walked over 2 miles from my apartment to the concert they had down at the bandstand in Central Park—and then I took a cab home." Everyone was smiling and nodding in approval.

"Well, that's wonderful," Rebecca said. Looking around the circle, she asked, "Are there any others?"

The man with the black-framed glasses spoke next. "Well, this won't hold a candle to Lindsey's spring, but. . . ." He paused, nodded to her with a smile, then took a deep breath.

"I'm messing with a fountain pen!" he said proudly. Murmurs of anticipation spread around the circle. He pulled a thick, golden pen from his shirt pocket and held it high.

"I got the idea when I saw this in a jewelry store window. It cost nearly 200 dollars. I'm still practicing with it. But I can write my name!" he said, laughing. "No, really," he continued in a serious tone, "It may seem like a small deal, but the case for the fountain pen as a spring is pretty major. I mean, it's everything! It's art. It's communication: genuine, personalized, physical communication. I'm going to do all my birthday cards with it from now on."

"And maybe you could get into calligraphy?" asked Rebecca.

"Definitely," he said. "In fact, I've put a little style into how I write my name. I'll show you later." He gave a little grin of pride.

As the group grew quiet, Rebecca looked around the room, "And what do we have in the way of sparks?"

In response, one of the young men described a project he was doing with several other members of the group, something about hiring teenagers in the neighborhood to develop artistic posters to be used in advertising for local businesses. Apparently, a little workspace had been set aside for them in a local grocery store. He said their biggest challenge was getting more teens into the activity—they only had three so far. "More money won't help," he said. "We've got to find ways to pique their interest. If any of you can think of something, please let us know."

Shortly before 9:00, as the conversation wound down, Rebecca said, "Well, everybody, thank you so much!" and stood up. The others rose and began collecting things and chatting. "Here's for next time, "she said, handing out a sheet to each member. "It brings up automobiles, Lindsey," she said to the woman who had given up her car. Turning to me, Rebecca said, "Well, I hope you got an idea about what BHB is?"

"Yes," I said cautiously, "but I have a lot of questions. For example, what's a 'spring' and a 'spark'?"

"Oh yes, of course that would be new to you," she said. "I'm sorry we didn't explain it."

"And," I continued, "I really would like get in touch with the head office of BHB, talk to the director. I'd really like to write an article. . . ."

Rebecca looked puzzled.

"Do you think I could meet the person who writes these BHB things?" I lifted the sheet that had the "Humility" prompt. "You got it from somewhere, right?"

"Well, yes, I did get it in the mail from a friend." Her manner seemed strangely hesitant, like she was hiding something. Then, speaking quickly, she said, "But listen, let's meet and go over all this. Right now, I have to be somewhere. I promised my daughter and her husband that I would babysit for them at 9:00 while they did their run." I made a mental note that Rebecca was a grandmother who lived near her children.

Rebecca quickly jotted her phone number in my notebook. "Be sure to call me," she said, patting my hand as she turned to go.

Shortly after, I also took my leave, thanking the members for their hospitality. Since they were relative strangers, I felt it would be awkward to ply them for information about BHB. I would just have to wait until I could sit down with Rebecca.

Well, I thought, as I pushed out the apartment house main door, this group is certainly a bundle of puzzles! I felt more curious than ever about the mystery of who started this organization and for what purpose. It clearly seemed to be challenging technology, challenging the whole direction in which the modern world was headed. There was a major story here, something the media would really be interested in. . . if I could get to the bottom of it.

Once I gained my seat on the Subway car heading home, I took out the document that the group had been discussing and studied it carefully. It seemed a little deep—almost like poetry. At least I saw how the reference to monkeys fit in.

11

On the weekend following the intriguing BHB meeting with Rebecca, I was plunged into a far more challenging drama. It was Saturday, May 23, the day we set aside for Niccole's doing without her smart phone.

Over the weeks that I had been getting to know her, implementing our exercises and challenges in the park, it was clear that Niccole was more than ready to put some space between herself and her phone. Indeed, if anything, she was becoming something of a zealot against phones—partly as a result of the indoctrination of the support group she was attending, no doubt.

In fact, one day in the park I became the censured party. During one of our walk-arounds, I took a call from an important customer, a call that went on a little longer than it should have. After I ended, Niccole turned and, poking her finger against my chest, said with play-acting sternness, "And *you're* supposed to be the doctor!"

We were just coming up to Cliona's cart. "Let's ask an independent authority to judge your behavior. Cliona," she said, turning to the smiling flower vendor, "do you think it's right for Jon to take a five-minute call while we're walking in the park? Is that polite?"

It was all in fun, of course. I was curious to see what the eternally beneficent Cliona would say. It seemed there was no way she could get around picking sides.

She gave a broad smile, hesitated a moment, then said, "Well, when you have such a handsome man and such a beautiful woman," she said, nodding to each of us in turn, "nothing should come between them."

"My, what a diplomat you are Cliona!" Niccole said. "You should work for the State Department!" It was a happy moment for us all.

So, Niccole was more than ready for the one-day phone denial experiment. She had several times raised the issue, asking whether I was really serious about the idea, and if so, when it should happen.

It seemed to me that this event should be a special, day-long outing, an outing away from the city and into nature, where we would see trees and birds, and that we should, of course, do it together. Thumbing through the *News* one morning, I spotted an ad for the Circle Line that seemed perfect. The next morning, I broached it to Niccole.

"How about we take a day trip up the Hudson River to Bear Mountain Park, on the boat?"

She grabbed my arm. "Yes! Yes! When do we go?" she gasped with excitement.

As I visualized it, this trip into the countryside ought to have been a straightforward expedition. According to the schedule, the boat took three hours to reach Bear Mountain, giving us about four hours to hike around the park, and then we would take the boat back to the City in the late afternoon. Niccole suggested, pointing out that since we were going through a rather formal ritual of renouncing the phone, that I should leave my phone behind too. I was a little uneasy, but saw no real problem in accommodating her.

When the day arrived, I packed up a picnic of Swiss cheese sandwiches along with two apples, and put this, along with bottles of Perrier and a little blanket, into my day pack. I met Niccole, as arranged, at Pier 83 in time for the 9:00 a.m. departure. We made up quite a crowd, some 40 to 50 people, gathering by the *Henry Clinton*, moving up the gangplank and giving the steward our tickets. Niccole and I were too interested in this novel mode of travel to remain in the main cabin and quietly consume the brunch that the waiters had laid out. We went up on deck and walked to the very front of the boat where, clinging to each other, we stood against the blasting breeze that the boat's speed created. (A crew member later told me that the boat's cruising speed was 18 mph.) The ship's white bow sliced and smashed through the water, throwing up a high wave; a few drops flicked up and spattered our faces now and then, giving us a delightful taste— you might say literally—of sea travel.

We zoomed under the George Washington Bridge, the great structure towering high above our heads. Niccole, looking at me with a broad smile, made a throwing motion with her hand, and I smiled and nodded, showing that I knew she was referring to George, the member of the Nanoelectronics group who threw away his phone from the bridge. A few seconds later, we saw the gray stones of the monastery tower at the Cloisters at Fort Tyron Park. These religious buildings and ancient walls always evoke for me the mystery of medieval Europe.

The time up the river passed quickly. We did return to the main cabin, having our fill of scrambled eggs and frosted croissants, and visiting with some of our fellow travelers. Just before noon, we reached the Bear Mountain dock. The captain said over the loudspeaker that the boat would leave to return to the city at 4:00 p.m., that we must be at the dock by that time. He added that if we missed the return trip our money would not be refunded. This same announcement was repeated five minutes later.

Our plan was to hike up the 2 miles of the trail—a segment of the Appalachian Trail, as we learned later—to Perkins Tower, and then take the shuttle bus back to the dock. The ascent was a delightful nature walk. We went past Hessian Lake and headed up the hill, remarking on the profusion of wildflowers, none of which we could name.

After about the third time that Niccole said, "Oh, I *wish* I knew what this is" as she fondled a blossom, I said, "Well, if I had my phone, we could just take a photo and let Mastermind tell us."

I was just being playful but Niccole gave me a reproving look. "We don't need that."

We were especially interested in a purple flower that filled up one whole side of a meadow, a little ocean of vivid color. Each flower had over a dozen bell-shaped blossoms hanging from a vine-like stem. In answer to Niccole's query about its name, I said, "Well, let's call it a 'purplebells' for the time being, and then we can look it up when we get home."

"Do you think I could pick one and take it home?" asked Niccole with a half-guilty smile.

"Well," I said, "they're going to be dead in another week, anyway, so I think God and the State of New York would forgive you." I adopted a formal tone. "I hereby authorize Niccole Evenson to pluck one purplebell flower for transport to New York City."

She giggled, plucked one stem, rolled it carefully in a tissue and put it in her purse.

It was mid-afternoon when we reached Perkins Tower with its spectacular view of the Hudson Valley, the silver band of the river twisting between the blue hills into the distance. Before we entered the tower, I went and checked with the shuttle bus driver about return times. He said that he would leave in 15 minutes and that there would be one more bus after that. This seemed to give us plenty of time to climb the tower and enjoy the view.

On descending from the tower, Niccole said she had to use the restroom, and I decided to do the same and we split up. We didn't make any plans for meeting in a particular place; we just assumed we would see each other in the parking area.

I went to the men's room and discovered a long line outside the door. As we had seen coming up the hill, the park was quite full on this early summer Saturday afternoon. We had passed scores of people—families, couples, tour groups—going both ways. There must have been hundreds in the tower area—all needing to use the bathroom of course. Finally—it must have been 15 minutes—I got my turn, and came back out just in time to see the shuttle bus driving away. There was no sign of Niccole.

In a few minutes, another bus pulled up. As I confirmed with the driver, his was the last shuttle bus of the day.

I thought it likely that Niccole had taken the previous shuttle bus back to the dock. I assumed that while I had been delayed at the bathroom, she had been waiting at the bus stop. When I didn't appear, I assumed she figured I had taken an earlier bus, and decided the best place to be certain of meeting me was back at the boat.

This hypothesis became increasingly plausible as the minutes passed with no sign of Niccole. When the driver said, "All aboard," I climbed in the bus.

At the dock, I rushed down the steps of the bus and looked eagerly in all directions: No Niccole! I went up onto the boat and inspected both cabins, carefully looking at each of the many passengers who were getting settled for the voyage back to New York. No Niccole!

I went back down the gangplank to the dock.

"We're leaving in just a few minutes," said the crew member standing by the gangplank. "You'll have to get on board."

Oh, what a mess! I thought.

Since that very first moment of doubt at the bus stop by the tower when Niccole didn't appear, I of course knew what was at the bottom of this muddle: no phones! As soon as she didn't show up, I could have called her and found out what was going on. Without our phones we were helpless.

"All aboard!" said the sailor at the gangplank, looking at me.

Since Niccole wasn't on the boat, it seemed obvious that I should not leave Bear Mountain.

"I'll stay here," I said to him. "I have to wait for someone."

The sailor shrugged, untied the ropes mooring the boat and went up the gangplank. He pulled the levers of the crane that lifted the gangplank and swung it to the side of the boat. The engines rumbled and the boat eased away, creating a wider and wider gap between the hull and the dock. Several of the passengers standing by the bow waved to me, and I felt duty bound to reciprocate, but there was not an ounce of cheer in my wave.

As the moments passed, I grew more and more uneasy. What on earth had happened to Niccole? Was she trapped somewhere, lost somewhere, attacked somewhere?

And what should I do? I kept asking the question as I paced in small circles around the pier. I kept reaching in my pocket for my non-existent phone. Without my phone, I could not call anybody for help. I could not call the police; I could not call a taxi. I knew I should not go anywhere, because this was the only place where Niccole knew to find me. I was trapped.

Anyway, I thought grimly as I paced in little circles on the dock, this exercise was proving to be a vivid demonstration of why phones are necessary.

After 20 minutes—the worst 20 minutes of my life—I saw a car approaching on the street alongside the pier, a blue-gray Toyota. It pulled to a stop, the passenger door opened, Niccole jumped out and ran to me.

Oh my, did we hug! It was lucky that nobody broke a rib.

"What happened to you?!" we both exclaimed, and then hugged again. And then, still echoing each other, we said at the same time, "I was so worried!"

As the exclamations and hugging subsided, Niccole said, "There was *such* a long line at the bathroom!" She shook her head. "It was the Superbowl! I had to wait an hour!"

As soon as she said it, I realized my mistake. I had failed to deduce that if the men's room line was long, it would be twice as long for the women's, and that's where Niccole had been held up.

"So when you weren't there and they said the last bus had gone, I didn't know what to do." She looked back at the driver of the car. "Anyway, it's a long story, but Elle here picked me up!"

Niccole was smiling enthusiastically as she drew me over to the car.

We poked our heads in the open passenger-side window. "Jon, this is Elle," she said, indicating the driver, a middle-aged woman with dark brown hair done in a long ponytail. Elle, smiling broadly, leaned over toward me with her hand outstretched and I leaned in the window and took it. Even from that first moment, I could sense that these two women had struck up a close, energetic friendship. It seemed like Niccole was introducing me to her favorite aunt.

"Here, let me get out and meet you properly," said Elle. She opened her door and came around.

"Actually, her name is really 'Elaine', said Niccole, "but everyone calls her Elle." Elle nodded at her with a smile. "Elle lives in the city. She's up here visiting her sister." Then Niccole turned to me.

"You have no idea how worried I was when I heard the last bus had gone and you weren't there," she continued, looking into my eyes. "I didn't know what to do! So finally, it seemed like the only thing I could do was walk down the road to the pier. I don't know how long that would have taken, but then"—she indicated Elle with a smile, "this lovely person came along and gave me a ride!" Elle smiled back. "She just stopped and said, 'Do you need a ride?'"

"Well, it's just so wonderful that it all worked out," I said. "Of course, now we've got the problem of how to get back to New York City."

"Oh, we've got that all figured out," said Niccole. "Elle is going to take us to the train station at, where. . .?"

"Manitou," said Elle.

"Manitou, and it will take us right back to Grand Central!"

"Well," I said, taking in a deep breath and turning to Elle, "That's very kind. I don't know how to thank you. . . ."

"Oh, heavens, it's no problem," said Elle. "Actually, it's been a delight to meet you guys."

With that, we got into the car, and Elle drove us to the station about 10 minutes away. We got out and said good-byes. After Elle and Niccole hugged, Elle said to her, "And be sure to let me know about the babysitting."

"Oh, I will, I will!" said Niccole enthusiastically.

It was after 9:00 p.m. when our train reached Grand Central. On the trip down, we caressed rather extensively. "We're going to get thrown off the train for this," I jested. Fortunately, the car was nearly empty and there was no one observing our antics.

As the slowing train clattered over the switches coming into Grand Central, Niccole looked up at my face with bright eyes. "Do you think it's possible that I could spend the night at your place?" She was tickling my tummy at the moment. We both understood this didn't mean her sleeping on the couch in my living room.

"Of course," I said, grinning.

"I mean," she said gaily, pressing her finger on the tip of my nose, "you have to verify that I don't touch my phone for the rest of the 24 hours, don't you, doctor?"

I gave her a gentle poke in the ribs that evolved into something else.

TAKING HUMAN BEING

12

We spent the night together in my apartment, had a leisurely late breakfast of almond croissants with raspberry ganache from La Bicyclette bakery, and went for a walk together to the 79th Street Boat Basin before Niccole went back on the Subway to her apartment in the Bronx.

'We spent the night together.' Such a simple phrase—but, it was the opening of a new world to me.

Through my teen years at Englewood High, I had, without realizing it, come to see physical relations with the opposite sex as something of a task. Exciting, engrossing, to be sure, but still, a realm centered on the task of overcoming natural inhibitions. The pattern began in the seventh grade, if I remember rightly, with a list of rungs to be scaled—just like Niccole had described back at our dinner date at the Shamrock Grill. Challenge number one was the first date, and then came more lines to be crossed: holding hands, the first hug, the first kiss. The language in my circle reflected this ladder-climbing orientation: "How far did you get?" was a standard question, as if this was a mountain to be climbed. A few grades later, it became, "Did you score?" Both boys and girls were rated according to how 'fast' they were.

As I've explained, I stood rather poorly on this scale, being on the shy and inhibited side. As the years passed, I eventually crossed the lines my companions had been crossing years before—and finally succeeded in "going all the way" as it was put. But the whole process had left me with a rather mechanical view of what boys and girls did together. Yes, it was fun, and yes, it was biologically necessary for the human species, but as I matured into adulthood, it was not a central interest in my life. This feeling of detachment was part of my image of myself as a natural bachelor.

The night with Niccole was changing that. There was an amazing chemistry between us that swept away the limited view of love-making that, without quite realizing it, I had assimilated. She had gone through a similar experience of battling high-school inhibitions, and also had been left with a cautious perspective. As we explained our backgrounds to each other—our awkward experiences, our feelings of shyness—our inhibitions drained away. We came to see ourselves as soulmates, and we took it for granted that we would repeat this process of intense, delightful exploration.

The Tuesday night following the Bear Mountain trip we had dinner with Asher at Piccola Cucina Ora, a get-together I had set up many days earlier. Of course, I wanted my boss to meet Niccole, who was becoming an important part of my life. In fact—not that I would tell him or anyone—I was having a love affair with this woman, an amazing love affair. A new sun had arisen over the flat panorama of my life, shining light into all its drab corners. I could sense that this new planetary force would, in due course, imply a lot of adjusting in my lifestyle and perspectives, but for the moment I was just basking in the joy of it.

The ostensible purpose of our little dinner gathering was to lay before Asher the outcome of his challenge, the 'bet' he made on that day when we observed Niccole engrossed on her cell phone in the park. Of course, he knew that I had been meeting with her about her phone problem. When I told him that she, too, had offered me $100 to help her stop using the phone for a day, his jaw dropped. "Doesn't the world work in mysterious ways!" he said. "Anything I can do to help, let me know."

My dinner invitation had another purpose, as well: perking up his social life. Asher doesn't get out that much. He's too much the philosopher, always reading books. I don't know how many times he's quoted Thoreau at me. He's nearly 60, unmarried and has never said anything about being in a relationship. I suspect that he had a bad one some time ago that he doesn't want to talk about. I felt this dinner would do him good.

When we came into the restaurant, he was already seated at our table, dressed, as usual, rather formally in blue tie and gray blazer. The air in the busy dining room was heavy with the aroma of pasta and garlic. Asher rose and greeted Niccole with a handshake.

"Jon has told me about you," Niccole said, speaking energetically. "I'm so happy to meet you at last."

We took our places on the red, cushioned chairs and straightened the silverware before us.

"So," said Asher, after studying her glowing face, "I guess there can't be much doubt that doing without a phone for a day makes a person happy!"

I hadn't told Niccole about the 'bet' and Asher's theory, but somehow, she understood the connection that he was alluding to, the idea that doing without a phone made one happier.

"Oh, it was a very happy day for me," she said emphatically.

"But it nearly was a disaster," I said.

Niccole giggled, and I let her explain the mix-up with restroom delays and the buses. "And then," she finished the story, "this wonderful woman came up in her car and gave me a ride down to the dock!"

At that moment, the waiter came and we gave our orders. I was surprised to see that Niccole ordered the braised squid. I wouldn't have guessed she would be that bold. I wondered if our expedition had encouraged a spirit of exploration.

After we handed back the menus to the waiter, I said, taking up the account of the bus-missing snafu, "It's a good example of why phones are necessary. I mean, if Elle hadn't come by in her car, we would really have been sunk! We were completely without any ability to communicate."

Niccole frowned, her first frown of the evening. "No," she said softly, looking down at the table. After a pause, she lifted her eyes and said it again, still gently but with more firmness. "No."

She looked at me. "There's another way to look at it"—she gently placed her hand over mine and gave a bright smile. "Not having a phone made the day what it was." Her brow furrowed as she worked out what she was trying to say.

"The way I see it is, we were certainly having a nice time, walking up the hill, seeing the flowers and all. That was fine. But then, when something went wrong, that made a chance for something really amazingly good to happen. When I was so worried walking down the hill and Elle stopped and said, 'Can I give you a lift?' I felt so relieved. It was an amazing sense of. . . joy!" She threw her hands in the air.

"And then, when we got to the bottom and I saw you standing there on the dock, I was"—she separated each word and marked each one with a gentle tap of her knuckle on the tablecloth—"So! Happy!" Her face was glowing. "It brought us together!" She looked into my eyes and squeezed my hand again.

I couldn't exactly argue with that, I admitted to myself. The risk and frustration of the episode had somehow brought us closer.

I glanced across the table at Asher, who was quietly beaming—perhaps with a touch of pride for being the one who originally set this course of events in motion. He gave a subtle nod in my direction.

The waiter returned and set steaming plates before us and we began to eat.

"Niccole makes a very interesting point," Asher said, pausing from eating. "If you eliminate all risk and danger, life can get pretty dull. If you let technology do everything, if you let it take away all challenges, you can end up a 24-hour couch potato."

"That seems a little extreme," I said. "I mean, this fork," I continued, raising mine in the air, "is technology. Are we supposed to eat with our fingers?" I realized as soon as I said it that I had chosen an example that would be much too provocative for Niccole, given her exuberant mood.

Smiling, she lifted her fork ceremoniously over the middle of the table and let it drop with a little twang on the white tablecloth. Then—looking gleefully into my eyes—she slowly stretched her right hand, fingers outspread, over her plate of pasta and squid. She tipped her head at me with an expression that said, 'maybe I should pick up this food with my fingers?'

"Bravo!" said Asher grinning.

I played the role assigned to me. I gently took her right wrist and placed the dropped fork in her hand. "I think we've had enough risks and dangers for one day," I said. We all laughed heartily.

Later the conversation turned to Niccole's job at the Everett furniture design company, and Asher asked how she liked it.

"It's been a little flat lately," she said, matter-of-factly. "But!"— she looked up—"I'm about to begin a second job!" She enjoyed our puzzled expressions for a few moments. "As a day care assistant!"

"Was that what you and Elle were talking about?" I asked, remembering the parting comments at the train station at Manitou.

"Yes," she replied. She turned to Asher. "Elle—the woman who picked me up coming down Bear Mountain—is part of a thing they call a 'manual community' over on East 107th Street."

"I've heard of those," Asher said. I certainly hadn't.

Niccole shrugged. "I don't really know what it's all about, but anyway, they have preschool children, and need somebody to help look after them."

"You mean, you're going to quit your job?" I asked.

"No, no. Certainly not now. The idea is, I'll be working at the community part time, in late afternoons, two days a week from 4:00 to 7:00 p.m., to try it out. I've arranged to leave Everett early on those days. Then after a few months, we'll see. I go over there for the first time next week."

After a moment, she added, "I'm really excited about it because it involves children." She looked at me and continued,

"When Elle first mentioned they needed a child care helper, I had to tell her that I had no experience with kids. She said it would be no problem. As I've thought about it since, I've begun to realize that children might be what I needed in my life, that maybe this was something I've been missing. I mean, I'm 27 and it's been years since I've even talked to a child."

"That's very interesting," said Asher, nodding. "I'd be interested to hear how it works for you."

"Oh, I will." At that point, Niccole excused herself to visit the ladies room.

When she was out of sight, Asher reached into his hip pocket and brought out his billfold. He withdrew a bill and dropped it on the table in front of me.

"There's your $100," he said. "Boy, did you earn it!" He looked me straight in the eye. "And you proved my theory, didn't you?" he said, basking in satisfaction. "About getting away from technology making a person happy. She is the happiest person in this whole restaurant!"

Smiling, I waved my hand at the bill. "No, no. I can't take any money for that," I told him. "It was a great experience. In fact," I lowered my voice, "it brought us amazingly close together."

"I can see that," Asher said with a wink. Nodding vigorously, he added, "She's really taken with you." I felt a little burst of pride.

The $100 bill remained lying on the table. We both knew it shouldn't be there when Niccole returned.

"I'll tell you what," Asher said. "You take it, but not to spend on yourself. Instead, use it to motivate someone else to achieve something worthwhile." He saw my hesitation. "There's no rush. Maybe it will be years before an opportunity arises. . ."

I saw Niccole coming around the corner from the ladies' room, grabbed the bill and slid it into my pocket.

". . . to spark someone onto a higher plane," Asher quickly finished as we looked up at Niccole.

She slipped into her chair. "Is somebody making a flight?" she asked, looking back and forth at us. "You were talking about planes. . .?"

"No, no," we said simultaneously. To cover the awkward moment, I asked Niccole, "Have you been able to look up that flower?" I turned to Asher. "We found this really pretty purple flower at Bear Mountain, but we don't know what it is. Niccole brought a stem of it home."

"No," said Niccole, answering my question. "And I'll tell you—I know it sounds strange—but I don't feel comfortable using the Internet to find out. Somehow, it seems more precious than that. What I really want"—she said, with an irresistible look of pleading—"is one of those old-fashioned flower identification books."

My broad smile and nod told her that she would soon have such a volume.

As we continued our meal, in one corner of my mind lay the memory trace that Asher had used the word "spark," a word that had a connection to one of the puzzles of the BHB meeting last Friday. But our conversation had plunged off into other directions too quickly for me to pursue this thread.

13

Three days later, I went to meet Rebecca for a late afternoon coffee. She offered to come downtown and meet with me near my apartment, but I insisted on coming up to Washington Heights where she lived.

My head was full of questions about BHB, about when it was formed, who ran it, and what this business of 'sparks' was all about. I wanted to start writing about it, but I didn't know where to begin. The Internet, as I had already learned, was completely blank about it, and I saw this conversation as a way to begin to gather some hard facts.

Rebecca was waiting for me at the top of the Subway stairs. Her ruddy complexion matched her bright pink blouse and set off her cheerful smile.

"Did you have to stand up all the way?" she asked me as we started walking.

"Well, yes, the train was pretty crowded," I replied. "But I'm a New Yorker and I can take it." She smiled at my jest.

Just before we reached the coffee shop, Rebecca tugged my arm to pause us, and pointed across the street. "That's the grocery where the boys are doing the artwork project that we talked about last Friday."

Above the store, a bright green and yellow sign said, "Sunshine Market." It looked newly painted. Underneath the name in smaller print it said, "Natural Foods for Natural People."

"So," I asked, "the kids make posters for this store, inside the store?"

"That store, and all kinds of other local businesses. There are over 20 businesses now that take their art."

I sensed that Rebecca wanted to show me the operation, but I thought it best not to take up time discussing it until I had cleared up my questions about BHB. "That's very interesting," I said, and then turned to continue our course to the coffee shop.

After we ordered at the counter and seated ourselves at a little table toward the back—we were the only customers at that late hour—Rebecca pressed her hands together and said with a gay smile, "Well now, how can I help you?"

"To begin with," I said, "I'd like to find out more about BHB." I looked at her. "I mean, what is its purpose? Who founded it? When was it founded? How many members does it have? Where is the headquarters located?" When she didn't reply immediately, I continued, "Things like that."

"Well," she said slowly, "I'm not really the best person to ask about those things. I know it has a lot of members, but I really can't say how many. . . ."

I saw I would have to simplify. "Why don't we start with your own membership. I suppose you pay dues to somewhere? Maybe you have a membership card that gives an address, something like that?"

She had a blank expression. After a moment she said, "I've never heard anything about dues. . . ."

"So you never paid them any money?"

"No, not that I can think of."

"And you don't get a newsletter or a magazine every month?"

"No, I've never seen one."

"The reason why I ask is I've gone online, and nothing comes up for BHB. I mean, how can that be?"

"Well, that's to be expected, isn't it? That an organization that questions modern technology would avoid using modern technology?" Her smile seemed to suggest she knew more than she was saying.

This was most puzzling! It seemed like this BHB was some kind of shadow organization, almost an underground operation. Of course, this sweet woman couldn't be a part of any kind of conspiracy. She was on the outside, just like me. Perhaps she was the kind of supporter the communists used to call "useful fools," fellow travelers who didn't really know what was happening behind the scenes. In fact, probably everyone in the group last Friday night belonged in this category. They were nice people, they meant well, but they didn't know what the organization was really up to and who was running it. I was pretty sure that somewhere behind all the vague cordiality there had to be a real organization with a real leader and some kind of agenda.

But for the moment, my investigation had hit a stone wall. Then I remembered the paper sheet. I pulled it out of my pocket. "This...." I waved it, letting it unfold. "Well, could I ask, where did you get this 'Humility' document that we used the other night?"

"Oh that? That essay was sent along by my friend Mark. I thought it would make a good prompt for our exploration. Did you find it interesting?"

"Well, yes, I did. But now who is Mark? Is he an official in BHB?"

"Oh, I doubt it. Mark Thurlow is a professor who lives in Brooklyn. He sent me that essay along with several others about a month ago."

"Do you think I could contact him?"

"Sure, let me give you his phone number." She took out a little address book and wrote a number down on a slip of paper which she gave me.

I took the piece of paper and carefully folded it into my billfold. At last, I thought, I have a specific connection to the BHB organization!

I wanted to continue the conversation, to try to unravel something more of the BHB puzzle, but I didn't want to appear to be "pumping" her, or seem like I mistrusted her—which I didn't. In my mind, she was as pure and honest as a child. After a few more moments of conversation—which got into her plans for a trip to the Catskills—I politely brought our meeting to an end. "Well, thank you so much for meeting with me," I said as we rose from the table.

She gave a broad smile. "If there's anything more I can do, please let me know. Oh, and by the way"—she opened her purse again and took out a folded sheet of paper—"this you should probably have," she said, handing it to me. "It's called 'Ease or Joy?' It's one of the oldest prompts that people have copied and recopied. It gives something of the overall thinking in BHB."[4]

After a little pause, she continued, "And I hope you will come to our circle again, a week from Tuesday? We really enjoyed having you."

[4] The text of this document is included in the Appendix.

"Oh yes, I will."

She walked me back to the Subway station, giving me a big hug on our parting at the top of the stairs.

I headed down the stairs, turned and gave her a wave. Only a few moments later, when I reached the Subway platform, it hit me that I had forgotten to ask her about springs and sparks.

14

I decided not to call Professor Mark Thurlow immediately. It seemed wise to work up a list of careful questions for him, first. If BHB really was a secret organization, I didn't want to appear to be too aggressive and put anyone on guard. I had to pretend to be just a pleasant, curious bystander.

I also thought it would be a good idea to sound out Carl Winston, who was an assistant editor at the *Times*. For many years, Carl and I had worked together as writers at *Wise*, before it folded. He went on to get a job at the *Times* and he served as my contact there when I had items to submit.

"So what's the name of this organization you want to write about?" he asked.

I carefully introduced the topic. "BHB—have you heard of it?"

"Never. What the hell does it mean?"

"Being human being." There was a moment of silence on the line. Then Carl responded, "What does it do?"

"That's what I'm trying to find out," I replied. "It has meetings where people talk—small meetings." When Carl said nothing, I went on, "It seems they are trying to be helpful to people."

"People helping people isn't news," Carl said drily.

I saw his point immediately, and realized that I had to convey the mysterious aspect of the organization, and suggest some aspect of danger to get the newspaper interested. "I know it sounds strange, but I think it may be a cover for some kind of conspiracy. They're up to something. I mean, all of a sudden, one morning they could have a sit-in somewhere, or topple a statue!"

"Hmmm." A note of curiosity had crept into Carl's tone. "Well, as you well know, if it bleeds. . . . What policies does it stand for?"

Carl's question was embarrassing, since I hadn't yet figured out the answer to it, but I couldn't admit that. I had to make it seem this was a dangerous, newsworthy group. "They're anti-technology militants, Carl. They're against electronics. Against machines—that kind of thing."

"Luddites, you mean? People who go around smashing factories?" he asked.

I figured it was best to go along. "Yea, maybe something like that." Then, thinking of Niccole and Nanoelectronics, I said, "They certainly have it in for smartphones. I think they may want to smash them with sledgehammers. But I have yet to interview their leader to pin down their overall positions."

"Well," he continued, "we could sure use some demonstrations against big corporations, for sure." His tone indicated that our conversation was over. "Keep your eye on it and come back when you know more."

"Sure will, Carl."

After I hung up, I had to admit to myself that I had gotten carried away a little to get Carl's interest. All the vibrations I had got about BHB pointed away from any kind of violence or disruption. Maybe I didn't know what the organization was for, but it seemed that the last thing people like Rebecca or Ginny would be involved in was any kind of public spectacle. In fact,

BHB was starting to feel like the opposite of an activist group. Instead of wanting to attract attention, BHB seemed to want to be unnoticed. But what would that make it? A 'passivist' group? I shook my head. This puzzle was getting deeper and deeper.

The next morning at the office just after 9:00 a.m. with my sheet of prepared questions before me, I took out my phone to call the professor. I had looked him up in Inforall. Mark Thurlow was a professor of microbiology at Columbia University, 63 years old, and the author of a book entitled *Prokaryotic Diversity*, whatever that was.

He answered on the first ring. "Thurlow here."

"Hello, Dr. Thurlow. I'm so glad I reached you. I'm Jon Jones. I'm a friend of Rebecca Nelson's. . ."

"Oh yes," he said. "How is Rebecca? I had a lovely dinner with her and her husband about a year ago."

"She's fine. In fact, she invited me to her BHB exploration the other night, and that's why I'm calling you, to find out more about the organization."

"Oh?" His tone seemed guarded. "Are you some kind of reporter?"

"Oh no," I replied. I wondered what made him suspect me so quickly. Had my tone of voice given me away?

"That's good," he said, "because BHB and reporters don't mix."

"Really? Why is that, if I may ask?"

"Well, it would take quite a while to give you the background, but let's just say reporters work with the hyper-figurative realm and BHB works with people."

That left me more puzzled than ever, but I thought it best to pretend that I understood, and agreed with him. It was obvious that I couldn't let my questioning sound like that of a reporter. I wanted to ask where the BHB documents came from, and learn about the location of the head office. But I saw that such direct questioning would trigger his defenses.

"Well, that's interesting," I began. "What I'm really calling about is the document called 'Humility' which Rebecca told me came from you. I found it so interesting that I wanted to find out if there was any more material on the subject. Can you tell me where it came from so I can learn more about the topic?"

"Sure, that's no problem. It came in the mail. I should have the envelope in the file. Just a minute." There was a pause as he put the phone down and went to dig out the address.

A wave of excitement surged through me. I was just seconds away from getting the address of BHB. My mind raced ahead. Even if the organization was hiding itself and refusing to meet openly with reporters, I could go to the office and surveil the entrance, make a note of who came and went, follow them, identify them, eventually interview them. I would not be just a reporter but a sleuth uncovering a mystery!

In a minute he was back on line. "Here's the address. Have you got a pen?"

"Yes. Ready."

"Charles Stephenson, Box 71, Bonners Ferry, Idaho, 83805. Does that help?"

It was like being hit with a bucket of cold water, but I kept up my front. I wrote it down. "Very good, Professor. Thank you very much."

"No problem," he said. "Feel free to call me if you have any other questions."

He was obviously ending the connection, so I could do nothing but say goodbye and hang up.

I looked up at the ceiling, a deep frown furrowing my brow. This seemed all wrong. I had expected an address of a New York skyscraper. Or perhaps the number of a marble building on a presidentially-named avenue in Washington, D.C. Instead, I got a post office box number in—after I finally found it on the map— what seemed like the most rural village in one of the most rural states in the country.

As I thought about it over the following hours and days, however, my sense of dismay faded, gradually overtaken by a feeling that perhaps, after all, there was something fitting about this address. As I had been learning already, BHB was not any kind of normal activist group. It was, in some strange way that I didn't yet understand, practically the opposite of one. So, it wouldn't have an address in a big city, with a big entrance door you could just walk in. Maybe my brain was running away with me, but I began to sense a certain validity about this address that Professor Thurlow had given me. What better place for the headquarters of an anti-organization organization than a village in Northern Idaho?

I began laying plans to uncover and meet the man who, I had to suppose, was the mainspring of the BHB organization, the man who was responsible for all these "essays" that were indoctrinating legions of followers. I decided I would set aside my two weeks of vacation in August to travel to this village in the Pacific Northwest.

The first problem was that Bonners Ferry was far from any regular commercial airport. The airport of Boise, Idaho's capital, in the far south of the state was over 400 miles away. Then I discovered that the Amtrak train route ran right through the town. I supposed I could have flown most of the way and then taken the train, but the idea of travelling all the way from New York City to Bonners Ferry, Idaho, by train had a certain charm that appealed to me.

Even though the planned trip was a month away, I went ahead and made the reservation, and also reserved a room at Ruby's Best Western in Bonners Ferry on the night of my arrival, which, the schedule said, should happen at 11:50 p.m. I could see myself that night, stepping off the train and walking through the still, dark shadows of the quiet town, perhaps even passing in front of the BHB headquarters on the way to my motel.

At the time, I had not yet fully grasped the implications of the fact that I only had a post office box number, not a physical address.

15

15

It was noon when Niccole and I met with Cliona for lunch at Holy Smokes, a little sandwich and barbeque shop at the edge of Tompkins Square Park.

Our lives had, in just a few weeks, surged into new channels and challenges. After the trip to Bear Mountain, Niccole began spending nights with me at E. 47th Street, and her apartment in the Bronx quickly became an absurdity. She terminated the lease and moved in with me in June. It took us the whole weekend, and three trips in my fully loaded Nissan to bring her stuff to my apartment. Boxes and bags cluttered the living room floor for weeks thereafter until it gradually got sorted out and stored (among other adjustments, I gave her the top two drawers of my dresser).

She had clearly gotten over her phone attachment. If anything, a neutral observer might say she had overreacted. She felt that our day at Bear Mountain was a turning point, just like George's moment of throwing his phone off the George Washington Bridge. She wanted to leave the device totally behind her. She realized that it wouldn't be fair to her friends, and especially for her mother in Pennsylvania, to go entirely off the phone. She had established a schedule of having it on, and making and receiving calls on Fridays from 7:00 to 9:00 in the morning. That's when she would visit with her mother and make a few necessary other calls. The rest of the time, if you called her, you got her voicemail.

She continued to attend meetings as an enthusiastic new member of the Nanoelectronics support group, enjoying both the fellowship of these new friends and encouraging newcomers who struggled with, as she kept putting it, their "addiction."

Knowing her attitude, I tended to keep my phone use out of her sight. Of course, she was much too considerate to criticize me about it. But I knew the subject was in the forefront of her mind, and that was beginning to make me sensitive about it as well. I made sure mine was off before going to meet her at Holy Smokes.

We had set up this lunch with Cliona so Niccole could describe her new part-time job with the children at Elle's community organization, and "explain how it's changing what I want out of life," was how Niccole put it that morning as she rushed off to work.

We were seated at one of the little green metal tables outside, on the brick court in the shade of the elm trees. Cliona left her flower cart parked by the curb.

"And so, tell us," Cliona asked, "how is this day care appointment working out?"

Niccole's face glowed. "It is amazing!" She shook her head. "Really! I had forgotten how amazing kids are! Let me tell you what happened on the first day," she said, pressing her spread fingers on the table.

"Elle—she's in charge of child care and schooling—met me in the lobby and took me up the stairs to the door of the nursery. Before we went in, she said to me, 'I've told the kids that you're a visitor, so that's the role you should play today. Ask questions.'

On this first day I was being used as a test, a kind of practice opportunity for the children to meet strangers.

"You can imagine I was pretty nervous," Niccole continued. "I had no idea how I was supposed to get along with these kids. They might be afraid of me and run away. I certainly expected them to be shy, probably too shy to talk.

"Elle pushed open the door of the playroom. 'This is Miss Niccole, children,' she announced—there were five girls and three boys. 'She's new here, so you need to show her the special things you have, and help her when she needs help.' Almost immediately this little girl, Tessa, comes up to me and pulls on my hand. She had on this lovely blue ballerina dress. 'Miss Niccole,' she says, 'would you like to read my Ichabod Icicle book?'

"She drew me over to the couch, sat me down and handed me a book. Then she climbed alongside, opened the book for me and started pointing to the pictures and explaining the characters in them.

"It was amazing," Niccole continued, "to be entertained by this precious little girl. *She* was babysitting *me*!"

"Isn't that sweet," said Cliona.

"But that was just the beginning," continued Niccole. "It turns out these kids—they're just 4 and 5 years old—have begun to learn to cook! I have no idea how the organization manages this. Elle said later that she will go over the techniques of their educational approach. It obviously emphasizes independence and making a contribution as early as possible. Anyway, a little later, this other little girl, Janelle, who had the cutest blond pigtails, comes up to me and says, "Miss Niccole, would you turn on the stove so I can boil an egg?' I learned that the children aren't allowed to turn the stove on—which makes sense, since that way an adult is supervising whatever cooking is going on."

Niccole went on to describe the cooking and the other tasks the children took up. "They've obviously developed some system for getting these kids to mature early."

I asked, "Did the kids have any phones?" I suppose I was making a bit of a tease, but I also was curious about the point.

Niccole gave me a stern frown. "Of course not," she said. Then, after a pause, she added, "In fact, you don't see phones in there—with anyone. They obviously have a policy about it, and about the whole electronic business—television and all. It's one of the many things I have to ask about."

"And did you find out what this so-called 'manual community' was all about?" I asked.

"Not really," said Niccole. "It seems they've taken over an entire apartment building. I guess it's kind of like a commune, with several dozen families living there. Elle mentioned there is a vegetable garden on the roof that the children help with. Most of the adults work outside the building, at regular jobs in the city. They pay some kind of rent, while the others who work for the community in the building, like Elle, are paid, somehow—I think. I really don't know how all that goes."

"Well, can you tell us the name of the organization?"

Niccole had a blank look.

"I mean, surely there's a sign over the entrance, saying "Sunshine Manual Community," or something like that?" When Niccole gave no answer, I continued, "Or a title on a letterhead?"

Niccole shook her head. "I didn't see anything."

It crossed my mind that this urban commune arrangement

had something of a BHB flavor to it, a guarded anonymity—which added to my curiosity.

"I can hardly wait to go back there on Thursday," Niccole said eagerly. She explained the arrangement was for her to work there Monday and Thursday afternoons. "You have no idea how appealing these children can be! I know it sounds silly, but they seem. . . magical! I didn't realize until yesterday how much I've been missing—by not being around children, I mean." She looked intensely into my eyes. "Until now, I've looked at children and having a family as something of a side issue, something that could happen or not. Now. . . ." Her expression tightened. "Now, it matters to me!" She gave me a firm nod, as if to say, 'So what do you have to say about that?!'

I didn't know what to say. Fortunately, Cliona eased over the awkward moment.

"I know exactly how you feel," she said, nodding emphatically. Cliona had three children, long grown up and now living away from New York. They did come to visit occasionally. The youngest, Riley, ran her own day care establishment in Brattleboro, Vermont, as Cliona had proudly told us. "It sounds like this community is something like my cohousing unit on East 7th Street."

This piqued my interest. "Cohousing? What's that?"

"It's a joint ownership apartment building. We have common spaces, and ways of getting together and helping each other out. I handle the childcare in the lounge once a week, on Thursdays. That's why I'm not at the park with my flowers then." After a pause she added, "But I think your community"—she looked at Niccole—"is more integrated than that, what with buying food for the kids and having a school of its own."

"I guess so," said Niccole. "I'm still trying to figure out the pieces."

The waitress brought our food, which distracted us for a few moments. Then Niccole put down her fork. "Now. To change the subject," she said, looking up and pausing to gather our attention. "Vetch!"

She enjoyed our amused puzzlement for a moment. "You know, that lovely purple flower we found at Bear Mountain?" She pressed her palm on top of mine. "I looked it up in the book you gave me"—it was *The Field Guide to Eastern Wildflowers*—"and figured it out. It's called Vetch."

"That's not a very attractive-sounding name," I said, laughing. "In fact, it's rather gross, rhymes with 'retch.'" Niccole gave me a play-acting look of scorn. "Frankly," I went on, "I think calling them 'purplebells' would be much better."

"Oh, vetch is a lovely flower," said Cliona. "Its only problem is that its stems aren't long enough for proper display in a bouquet. I would never be able to sell it."

"Well, the name may not sound good," said Niccole, "but it's a very wonderful plant. It's not only beautiful. It's a legume that adds nitrogen to the soil, so it builds the soil. And it makes a nutritious feed for cows."

"By the way Cliona," I asked, "Where do you get your flowers to sell? Surely you don't raise them?"

"Oh no, of course not," she replied. She paused to draw up each sleeve of her bright pink blouse. It was getting rather warm in the park now. "In fact, it's odd that you should be talking about that community of yours because I get my flowers from something like that. They work out of an apartment building on 69th Street."

"Do they raise them on the roof?" I asked, thinking of the garden at Niccole's community.

"I don't think so, at least not mainly. What they've told me is they have some type of farm in New Jersey. They have a little refrigerated pickup truck they bring them over in."

"One thing I don't understand," I said to Cliona, "is how your prices can be so low. Surely, it must cost a lot to get flowers from New Jersey?"

Cliona gave one of her beatific smiles. "Well, it doesn't," she said. To dispel my questioning expression, she elaborated. "They say they are not raising the flowers to make money. In fact, the wages for the members are set at $2.00 an hour. I've asked about that, several times. 'It's a spark, Cliona.' That's what they say, whatever that means. But they seem very positive about it."

I thought, there is that word again, 'spark'! Apparently, this community Cliona is dealing with has some connection with BHB. Was this another branch of this conspiracy-like entity? I reminded myself that I needed to set up another meeting with Rebecca as soon as possible.

Since we were on the topic of Cliona's flower business, I decided to ask about another aspect that I'd been curious about, the way her prices were always in round numbers.

"By the way," I said, "do you charge sales tax?"

Cliona's cheerful countenance abruptly faded. She gave me a nervous look.

"I'm sorry," I said. "It's none of my business, of course."

There was a pause. Cliona looked at us, her brow furrowed. "It's just much too complicated for me, that tax business," she said in a low voice. "I'm sorry but I just couldn't figure it out. I would have to stop doing the flowers completely." A look of pain crossed her face.

She looked enquiringly back and forth at our faces. "I hope you're not mad at me. You don't think I'm a bad person?"

"Oh, of course not, Cliona!" said Niccole. She rested her hand on Cliona's shoulder. "You are a saint and we love you!"

I put my hand on top of Niccole's. "You do what you think is right, Cliona," I said, looking into her eyes, "and it will be right with us."

"Oh, thank you!" Cliona face flushed with relief.

"So anyway, it sounds like Cliona's flower supplier is another manual community," I said. "They probably have a little school there, too, come to think of it."

"I think they do," said Cliona. "At least they have some very helpful children who bring the flowers to my cart."

* * *

Later that afternoon at the office, my mind ran back to that very significant look Niccole gave me when she said how much she had missed being around children. It raised the marriage flag, of course, a topic I'd been wrestling with since Niccole had moved in. It reopened the whole picture of my life, of who I was, what I intended to be.

Before meeting her, I had settled into the idea that I was to be a bachelor, a free and independent spirit the way an aspiring writer should be. No suburbia for me! After starting to live with her, this picture really didn't change at first. After all, famous writers had lady friends, paramours to join them for the raucous, all-night sessions in the speakeasy. So, I was still fitting the model.

But as the days passed, the issue of Niccole and marriage kept creeping higher in my field of view, seemingly there every time I turned around. My mother, for example, repeatedly alluded to the point. I had mentioned to her in a call that Niccole had moved in with me at E. 47th Street and since then she always brought it up when we communicated. "And how is Niccole?" she asked in our last call, her tone indicating that this was not a perfunctory query but that Niccole was very important to her. After I reported on our latest activities, she said, "Well, that's so wonderful! Of course, your father and I are very interested in your plans." I didn't want to introduce a sour note by demanding, "What plans!?" I just said that things were "very busy."

And then there was pressure from Edith, Niccole's mom. Niccole had told her about me, and, overhearing bits of their phone conversation last Friday, I knew Edith had me in her sights, so to speak. In the bedroom I could hear Niccole saying, "No, he doesn't"—pause—"Of course he does, mom!"—pause—"I'm sure he wouldn't."

After Niccole said goodbye she came into the kitchen. "What don't I do?" I asked her. She gave me a serious look. "Mom was asking if you drink. Her friend Mary Louise Kamper recently lost a husband in a drunk driving accident—it was his second accident, as a matter of fact. So, it's very much on her mind." Niccole paused.

"She really wants to meet you," she continued, speaking gently but seriously. It suddenly occurred to me that Edith's idea was to look me over as husband material. Hmmm.

As I mulled the point over in the ensuing days, it became increasingly clear that a visit to Edith would be kind of an exploratory step toward marriage. But just exploratory, I kept saying.

And besides, there was the fact that I had, in Niccole, an amazing woman, much too precious to part with. As far as I was concerned, we should continue to live together. If it made other people happy to call this living together 'marriage,' why should I be so hung up on a word?

16

The following week, my suspicion was confirmed about BHB being involved in the manual community where Niccole had her child care job.

We were having supper on Thursday evening after she had finished her second week there. She was bubbling with enthusiasm, could hardly stop telling me about the activities. She had fallen quite in love with the children. I jokingly suggested that this was becoming her play group, and she cheerfully agreed. "Being with the children has woken up my life."

Elle had explained to her the group's philosophy of child-rearing. "The whole key to it," Niccole said, "is consequences. Letting the children find out for themselves what happens when they do something they shouldn't." She giggled. "Last Thursday, we burned the muffins!"

"What! How could that happen?"

"Cayden was in charge. He had done a wonderful job mixing the batter, filling the muffin tin, and setting the timer. But then, he got involved in playing Chutes and Ladders with Ned, and when the alarm went off, he didn't pay any attention. Oh, he heard it—and Tessa pointed out to him that the alarm had gone off. But he was just caught in this other distraction—you know how kids can be.

"Fortunately, Elle had told me about their philosophy of

letting children learn from experience, or I would have removed the muffins myself. But I understood there was a learning lesson here—and so did the older children. We were all looking at each other with knowing smiles as the burning smell started to come out of the oven. Finally, Cayden registered our concern and the smell, and put it all together and jumped up. 'What should I do? What should I do?' he asked frantically.

"I helped him focus, getting him to turn off the oven, gather pot holders, and carefully open the door. After he had put the smoking pan on the stovetop, he was in tears and pulled at my hand. 'I'm sorry, I'm so sorry!' he kept saying. I knelt down and took him in my arms and gave him a big hug. He's so precious!

"After the muffins had cooled, I encouraged him to dig out the burnt pieces, and we had"—Niccole giggled—"what we called, a 'burnt muffin party,' putting butter and honey on the less-burned pieces. The children were very gay about it, saying that burnt muffins had a neat taste—which is somewhat true. I found the bits surprisingly tasty, especially"—she added with a guilty smile—"with honey."

She was in such good spirits that I didn't want to sound critical, but I felt I had to make the obvious point. "But doesn't this approach seem inefficient, even wasteful?" I said. "Look at all the extra work it involved! I mean, just cleaning that muffin tin must have been an enormous job!"

Niccole gave a little laugh. "We couldn't clean it! It had to be thrown out, and when Elle came in—the smell of the burning muffins was all over the building—she told the children they would have to do without a muffin tin for the time being because the kitchen supplies money for that month had all been spent.

'One of the consequences,' Elle quietly said to me, winking. Well!"—Niccole was obviously enjoying recounting this dramatic moment—"as soon as Cayden heard that, he jumped up and said, 'I'll pay for a new one with my own money'—the children earn money from chores like working in the roof garden. As a matter of fact, some of them have quite considerable savings."

Niccole refilled her wine glass. "So anyway, now we're planning a muffin tin shopping expedition."

"But still," I said, "that seems a pretty inefficient way to teach kids to cook."

She furrowed her brow, thinking hard. "There's more to it than that. Efficiency can't be everything. Challenges, crises, mistakes. Like Asher said, they can add to human experience." She gave me a meaningful nod. Of course, I knew she was thinking how our Bear Mountain fiasco turned out so well. She continued, "But I understand what you're saying. It can seem something of a puzzle."

"Speaking of puzzles," I asked, "have you been told this group's name?"

Niccole shook her head. One of the many unknowns about this organization was its apparent lack of a name. This gap bothered me because it rather undermined my idea of trying to write a story about it for the papers. After all, the most important thing about any organization is its name—at least when it comes to publicizing it. You can't write a story that says, 'There is an unnamed organization that does interesting things.' You have to say, 'The Rainbow Cooperative does A, B, and C,' or 'The East Harlem Creative Association does this or that.'

I pursued the point. "Well, perhaps you could ask someone about it. It must have a name, or at least a clear reason for not having one."

"Okay, I will," she said. "By the way, they *do* have BHB groups over there, three of them as a matter of fact."

"Really?" I said, but I wasn't surprised.

Niccole started to stand up to leave the table. Then she stared at me and sat down hard. "This could be your book! Right?"

When I didn't answer immediately, she went on. "I mean, non-fiction, a non-fiction bestseller!"

I was amazed that she was so attuned to my writing ambitions and the direction I was heading. "Well," I said slowly, "as a matter of fact, I have been thinking along these lines. I think there is a real exposé possible. BHB is some kind of hidden group, maybe a conspiracy. In fact, I'm planning a trip West on my vacation to see if I can get to the bottom of who's behind it."

"Oh, that'll be wonderful. Yes, it's such an interesting organization!" After a pause, she went on. "They also have a branch in New Hampshire."

"Really?"

"It's a kind of farming community. They call it The Farm. People go up there, sometimes for just a month, some for a year, or they even decide to live there indefinitely."

"Do they raise their own food and things? Do they go around in horse-pulled buggies, like the Mennonites?" I asked. It was becoming clear that this organization was more extensive than I had imagined.

"I don't know about that. I do know they supply a lot of the food we eat. Practically every week, they bring a truck load down from New Hampshire. It was tomatoes and celery yesterday." Niccole's voice took on a dreamy tone. "It must be neat for them to be away in the country, working in their own gardens in the hills.

"Actually," she continued, with a touch of pride in her voice, "I've joined one of the BHB circles. I went to one for the first time after my babysitting today. It's the circle that looks to explore spiritual ideas."

"Wow, that's interesting," I said. "You mean God and stuff?"

Niccole nodded.

"And are they for him or against him?" I was jesting, but also curious.

"Well," she said, giving me a seductive smile, then coming around the table to put her arms around me from behind. "Are we sure it's a 'he?'"

I grinned. This girl is so clever!

She continued, speaking softly, running her finger around my face, "I brought the handout for you to read. But not now. I don't want you to get all intellectual so late in the evening. It's way past our bedtime."

The next morning at breakfast, after Niccole had left for work, I poured myself a second cup of coffee and studied the document she had brought home. The title was "Proofs of God" and it had the BHB initials at the bottom. It seemed thought-provoking, making the point that beauty, or rather, our love of beauty, could be considered a proof of a "transcendental reality." But it wasn't clear whether the person who had written it was advocating for an existing organized religion, or wanted to found a new one.

The document added to my curiosity to get to the bottom of the BHB business and confront the man who was behind it all, this Mr. Charles Stephenson in Bonners Ferry, Idaho.

17

"I'm worried about her."

Niccole had just finished what had become her regular Friday morning phone call to her mother in Warren, Pennsylvania. As she had told me, Edith had been a widow now for over a year after the death of Niccole's father, and she had not adjusted well, was not getting back into life. Niccole made the call from the bedroom, leaving me at the kitchen table, but I overheard a few words when she raised her voice, especially, "Mom, you really, really should stop doing that!"

When she came out from the bedroom, I set my cup down. "Is something wrong?"

"Not especially, but she sounds very down. And she isn't getting out. The only thing she does is church on Sunday, and it sounds like it's a very minimum level of contact. She leaves right after the service." Niccole shook her head and sighed.

"What was it you told her to stop doing?"

"Television! She goes on about the different shows. Make Your Life something, The Jensens—or Johnsons, whatever. She's spending her entire day in front of it. It's not healthy!" She bit her lip and frowned.

"Why don't we go visit her?" I asked.

Niccole looked up, a bright, eager smile on her face. We both understood that in making this suggestion, I was taking a small but important step toward a more serious relationship.

"Oh, she would love that!" she said, her eyes lighting up. "We'll see if we can do something to pull her out of her funk."

We arranged to make the trip on the July 4th weekend, to give us an extra day.

We started early, setting out in my Nissan at 6:00 a.m. to beat the traffic, taking sandwiches and a thermos of coffee to enjoy on the road. A bright rising sun gave a sparkle to the cars and trucks flashing past us in the oncoming lanes on the highway.

"We probably should sleep in separate rooms." Niccole made this remark out of the blue as we cruised down the New Jersey Turnpike.

"Uh?" I wasn't clear about what point she was making.

"Mom is rather old-fashioned. I think she'd feel uncomfortable about, well. . . you know?"

"You mean she doesn't know we're living together?"

"No, I've told her that. She knows. I had to tell her when I changed my mailing address."

"So...?"

"Well, this is her own house. I think she'd feel responsible, like she was approving of, well. . . ."

"Sex before marriage," I said, finishing her sentence.

"Something like that." I glanced over at Niccole. She was smiling contentedly, feeling that her point was made.

The car cruised along, passing through New Jersey's swampland of mud flats and cattails. High buildings rose in the far distance, Newark, probably.

"Isn't that a little hypocritical on our part?" I asked.

Niccole reached over and massaged my right shoulder. "If you love people, sometimes you have to be willing to pretend for appearances."

"Hmmm."

* * *

We had no problem getting on the Pennsylvania Turnpike and cruising across the state. The challenge came after leaving that highway at DuBois, and taking the tangle of secondary roads through fields and farms to Warren. It was some combination of Route 255, then Route 219, and then something else. I was completely dependent on Niccole's memory of the area.

Warren was not the farming village that had somehow formed in my mind's eye. It had paved streets, and no horses tied up in front of saloons. It had brick buildings downtown, even one bank building on a triangular corner that was five or six stories high.

We pulled up at Edith's home just before 3:00 p.m. She greeted us on the front porch, enveloping Niccole in a hug. "I've been watching for you all day!" She was small in stature, not even as tall as Niccole, and quite thin. Her hair was a dark brown, which might have been dyed, but I'm no expert about these things. She greeted me with a big smile. "Is it all right if I hug you?" she asked, as she did so.

"I think it's quite legal in the state of Pennsylvania," I quipped.

"Oh, isn't he clever!" she said, turning to Niccole, smiling.

"That's what I think, too," Niccole replied. They both beamed at me.

We entered the hall, carrying our bags. Edith said to Niccole,

"You're in your room, of course, and I've made up the bed in the study for Jon." Niccole gave me a firm look that said, 'Now, don't tease her about it.'

Our visit progressed in a quite normal, and I would say happy, fashion. The house was fairly neat and tidy. Niccole told me later that she was surprised at how clean it was. "Obviously," she said, "the fact that you were coming motivated her to make the place presentable." We had all our meals, including breakfast, on the large dining room table. Edith insisted on doing all the cooking, but she allowed Niccole to do the washing up.

I did see in the living room a wide screen TV and a purple armchair with TV schedules and guides resting on the coffee table in front. The seat of this chair was deeply pressed and wrinkled, but I didn't see Edith watch any TV while we were there.

The three of us took a number of walks around Warren, with Edith as an enthusiastic, well-informed guide. After supper on the first day, she took us to Commons Park that runs alongside the—surprisingly wide—Allegheny River. The park is especially known for many species of unusual plants tended by the local garden society, and statues of political and military figures including The Soldiers and Sailors Monument of the Civil War, a towering structure. I was surprised to discover that Warren is actually quite an old town, founded in 1795, according to the plaque at the park's entrance.

"I always think that horse is too fat," Edith said, pointing to the statue of a civil war general. It was true, the horse he sat astride was as wide as a Clydesdale pulling a hay wagon, not any kind of elegant stallion.

"It looks like they both have been drinking too much beer," I quipped.

The really interesting part of our visit took place on Sunday, at the United Church of Christ, where Edith was a member. We went with her to attend the 10:00 a.m. service. After it was over, the congregation moved to the fellowship hall for the coffee hour. There were about 50 or 60 people in the wide, low-ceiling room, picking treats off the serving table, and sitting at round tables, mingling.

We had found a table and Edith was chatting with the woman on her left while I sat quietly beside her. Niccole was off getting a piece of cake, I thought. It turned out she had been much busier than that.

She came back to the table, her eyes sparkling with excitement. She bent down beside me and whispered into my ear, "If anybody asks, you've been dying to learn to play pickleball all your life!" She sealed this message with a firm nod of her head.

In response to my look of perplexity, she whispered in carefully-measured syllables, "Just. Say. It!"

I shrugged, intrigued by this strange command.

Niccole shifted her attention to her mother and the woman she was conversing with. "Do you want some cake, Mom? Mildred?" she asked, and without waiting for a clear reply, she moved away toward the serving table. I gathered that this question was an excuse to cover up the real reason for her visiting our table.

Several minutes passed. Then Niccole came back, leading an older man by the arm. He was neatly dressed—one of the few men in the room wearing a jacket. He was slender, of athletic build, and had a kindly smile.

"Jon," said Niccole, "this is Rick Watson. He's the organizer, and an instructor, of the Warren Pickleball Association." She paused slightly, nodding toward me, as if expecting me to say something. When nothing happened, she continued, "He's a pickleball coach, teaching people how to play." Her tight little nod toward me said, 'Speak!' I finally made the connection.

"Really?!" I said, with a bit of play-acting drama. "I've been dying to learn how to play pickleball."

"Well," he said, his part obviously well-rehearsed, "I could give you a lesson this afternoon." Niccole continued staring at me, giving tight, tiny nods.

"Well, uh, that would be great," I said. "Where. . .?" I trailed off.

"Actually, for a lesson, I need two people," Rick said. "We have to have one on each side of the court. Another beginner." He looked around, his eye falling on Edith. "Would you like to help this poor boy out?" He gave her a warm smile.

"Well, I. . . I. . . don't know anything about. . ." said Edith, her voice trailing off.

"Oh, Mother, please!" said Niccole, putting an arm around her shoulder. "Jon would be so grateful!" As she said this, she gave me an intense little nod. I caught the cue, and began to grasp the larger purpose of what was going on.

"I really would, Edith," I said, looking at her pleadingly. "For years, I've been saying, 'I've got to learn to play pickleball,' and I've never had the chance."

"Well, heavens, if it means that much to you, I suppose I could," Edith said to me. "But couldn't Niccole. . . ?"

Niccole interrupted quickly. Obviously, she had anticipated

this issue. "But I can't, Mom. I've got this sore right elbow and I can't swing a racket. It would injure it."

Edith shrugged, then gave a little smile. "Well, all right then, to do Jon a favor, I'll try it, but I have to tell you, I'm going to be terrible at it!" Rick put his arm gently around her shoulder in reply. "You'll do just fine!"

The 'lesson' took place at 4:00 p.m. in a big covered court facility with a high metal ceiling. It was clear from the beginning that Edith was the center of Rick's attention. He gave her encouraging comments at every turn. We began with Rick tapping gentle shots over the net for each of us to hit back. Actually, pickleball is quite an easy game, much less demanding than tennis. The rackets are short paddles, and the balls are spongy 'nerf' balls. The court itself is about half the size of a tennis court. So, everything is about one-third the difficulty of tennis: the distance you have to run to get the ball, the strength you need to hit the ball, the speed of the ball when it comes at you. It's really a perfect game for people as they get older, and Edith seemed to be taking to it very well.

After Rick explained the rules, he set Edith and me up in a friendly game, while he served as referee and ball-getter. She seemed to enjoy it immensely, laughing when she mis-hit the ball, and cheering when she hit it well and won a point against me. I suspected it might have been the first time she had actually used her body energetically for the past year.

Rick concluded the session after only half an hour of play, wisely I think, to leave us wanting more.

"Well, that was an excellent introduction to the game, Rick," I said. "Thank you. I'll have to look up a pickleball court in New York."

"You do that. It's one of the best ways to stay in shape. And, Edith," he said, turning to her, "would you be interested in joining our league?"

"Well, I think that would be very nice, if you will have me," she responded happily. He explained the dues, and gave her a paper with playing times and phone numbers. "I'll give you a call about the Thursday session," he said to her as we left.

Niccole was almost breathless with excitement when we returned. It was clear she had been thinking of nothing else during our absence. "How was it? How did it go?"

"Fine," Edith said. "Rick suggested I play with the Thursday group, and I agreed. Mabel Giddings is in that. Rick thinks maybe she would work out as a partner."

"We actually played an entire game," I reported.

"Jon won, I'm afraid," Edith said with a smile. Then she added, "But at least I learned to stay out of the kitchen."

In answer to Niccole's puzzled look she explained. "The kitchen is the section of the court close to the net. If you're standing there, you're not allowed to hit the ball back on the fly. So, it's best not to stand that close to the net." After a pause, she said, "Rick is an excellent teacher. He makes everything seem so easy." She gave Niccole a careful look that suggested there was something more about Rick being left unsaid.

Niccole gave a little smile and changed the subject. "Well, I'm making an omelet for you hungry players. I'm just now putting the eggs into the pan, so it will be ready as soon as you've washed your hands."

We left to return to New York early the next morning, both of us hugging Edith out on the driveway before we got into the car. Once we were well under way, Niccole brought up the pickleball. "I'm just so glad we got her started on that! It really will get her out."

"And give her some exercise," I added.

"Of course." Niccole was silent for a few minutes. "And you know, something could happen with Rick. I think she's got an interest there."

"Well, he certainly seems like a nice guy."

"Oh, he's a gem. He's behind all kinds of constructive, helpful things in Warren."

We drove along the Turnpike, the rising sun in the east ahead of us.

"Of course, there was a bit of dissimulation involved," I said.

"What do you mean?" I don't know whether Niccole was feigning innocence or had forgotten how the pickleball arrangement got started.

I gave her a knowing smile. "That I'm—me!—dying to learn to play pickleball? And you, with your so-called sore arm."

"Oh, that." Niccole looked at the road ahead, smiling confidently. There was not a trace of guilt.

"So, we had two lies, one you told and one you made me tell." When she didn't say anything, I went on. "Of course, it's a little difficult to decide who's the guilty party. You for ordering me to lie, or me for obeying your orders." I reached over and gave her shoulder a pinch.

After a few minutes, she said, with a little laugh, "I guess it's a case of love justifying bending the truth."

"Hmmm."

After a few more miles I gave her a little sideways glance. "Well, at least we'll be able to sleep in the same room tonight."

18

A week after we returned from our expedition to Warren, the mystery about the name of Niccole's manual community deepened. She had just returned to the apartment from her afternoon child care stint there.

Dropping her overfilled bag on a kitchen chair she said, "I finally got around to asking Elle about this lack-of-a-name business."

"And?"

Niccole opened both hands, signaling bewilderment. "Well, she hemmed and hawed, and then she finally said, 'It's complicated.' She said it would be best for me to talk to Horace since he has been with the group longest and could give me a full answer."

"So I went to Horace—I know him since he does the purchasing of school supplies and cooking things. I told him about you, and your interest in writing about the community, and that you needed to know the official name of the organization.

"He got very serious. He ran his hand through his hair and said, 'It's complicated.' Niccole frowned. "This seems to be a very popular expression with these people."

"Indeed it is," I said. "I can't figure out what they're trying to hide."

"Well, that's kind of what Horace said. He said, 'The fact is, we don't want publicity.' When I asked him why not, he said again, 'It's complicated.' And then he said for you to come and talk with him. He gave me his telephone number for you to set up a visit." She handed me the slip of paper.

I tucked it safely away with my other BHB materials. There wasn't enough time to arrange this interview before I set out for Idaho, so it had to go on a back burner for the time being.

I had, however, been able to set up another meeting with Rebecca in Washington Heights and went up there in the early evening two days later. The summer had been warming up since early July and we were now in the middle of one of New York's famous heat waves. The Subway platform felt like an oven, having absorbed the heat radiated from the sunbaked street above. Inside the train, it seemed just about as hot, even though the air conditioners were blasting like mad. They were probably defective, I guessed, their refrigerant depleted after working so hard for days on end. When I climbed the stairs to the street in Washington Heights, my shirt was drenched with sweat. I noticed little tar bubbles oozing out of the asphalt on the street, and I had to take care not to step on them.

I felt enormous relief stepping into the air conditioning of the Humble Hummus Grill on 183rd Street. I spotted her in a booth at the far corner. She rose and waved me over.

Rebecca looked different this day. She had on olive-colored khakis and her face had an unusual energy. "What's up with you?" I asked. "Did you just win the lottery?"

"Oh, you can tell? I didn't realize it was so obvious." She

paused. "I'm going to the Catskills—you know, the trip into the mountains I told you about. It's tomorrow!"

"So where do you go—Kingston, Monticello?"

"Oh no. It's a place you've never heard of: Neversink, in Sullivan County. It's a three-night camping hike! We sleep out in tents and everything." She paused. "Actually, it's been quite an effort for me to bring myself to this idea. I'm very scared about bears—have been ever since I was a little girl. That's why I've always been afraid to camp out."

"So what made you decide to. . .?"

"I guess my husband put his finger on it. He said, 'Are you going to die afraid of bears?' And I saw he had a point. I'm 63. I only have one life. I wouldn't want to say, at the end, that I'd let this fear rule my entire life. So anyway"—she smiled and gave a firm nod of her head—"if I'm eaten by a bear, so be it!"

I gently touched her arm. "Of course, that won't happen!"

"I know, I know." She gave a little laugh. "Everyone says there's never a problem with bears. Bears are supposed to be very shy."

"Who arranged this tour?"

"It's organized by a BHB group in the Neversink area. They got the idea of giving city slickers a taste of the forest and a hiking challenge."

"Well, I can hardly wait to get your report on it," I said. "It might be something Niccole and I should try."

I started to open my notebook. "By the way, I'm going on a trip myself, a week from Saturday." I let a little pause develop for dramatic effect. "To the village of Bonners Ferry in Idaho—by choo-choo train, actually."

"Oh, my goodness!"

"I'm going to meet the man who started the BHB!"

"Really?"

"Yes, his name and address were given to me by your friend in Brooklyn, Professor Thurlow."

"That's nice." Her tone was patient, non-committal.

"Well, this man—his name is Stephenson—he is the one who writes the BHB documents," I said triumphantly. "I think he's the founder and head of the organization."

"Really?" Rebecca said again. Her expression continued to express a degree of uncertainty. I assumed that she was skeptical—as I had been—that this central figure in the organization should be located in such a far-away, rural location. I decided not to pressure her to elaborate on whatever misgivings she might have, but instead turned to the topic I wanted to discuss.

"So, now," I said, looking at my notebook, "let's get to this matter we've been putting off for so long. Springs and sparks." I looked up. "This has come up in all of the BHB meetings I have attended, with people mentioning activities they were doing, but I am still unclear about the underlying theory."

Rebecca smiled, but seemed content to let me speak on.

"I mean, let's start at the beginning. How do you define a 'spring' and a 'spark'?" When she didn't answer right away, I continued, "I know it's getting people to do interesting, creative things, but what's behind it?"

Then I added, with a grin, "And if you say, 'It's complicated' I'm going to scream." We both laughed.

Rebecca spread her hands out against the table. "Point well

taken. It's one of those things that, you know what they are, but it's hard to put it into words." She paused, taking a deep breath, then continued.

"You're right: it's getting people to do interesting, creative things. A 'spring' is when a person tackles a new challenge. He springs out of his rut, you might say. A 'spark' is when somebody gets someone else to tackle a challenge. In other words, he is the spark that gets someone else out of his rut."

"But is it just any kind of different, helpful thing?" I asked. "For example, would giving a beggar a dollar be a spark? Would my serving myself a dish of nice-tasting ice cream be a spring?"

"Oh, you're so analytical!" Rebecca said, smiling and nodding her head for emphasis. I felt a little twinge of pride at her compliment. She went on, "You're right, it isn't just any kind of new activity, or helping another person. Your examples would not really fit being a spark or spring." After a pause, she continued, "It ties in with technology. At BHB we have the idea that technology is, well, not the enemy, exactly, but something to watch out for, something to guard against."

"I've seen that," I said. "So, are you saying that springs and sparks are acts of doing without technology? Like, if I just throw my microwave oven in the trash?"

Rebecca laughed. "No, no. It has to be creative." She frowned in frustration, seeking for some way to explain this apparently subtle issue. Then her face brightened. "Neversink! Of course. That is a perfect example of a spring! We're going to hike, which is doing without the technology of transportation, and we're going to sleep in tents, which is using a more primitive system of shelter. That's exactly it!" she said proudly. "And"—she opened her hands, looking at me triumphantly—"for the Neversink BHB circle that has organized the expedition, this is a spark. They are helping other people—me—get out of ruts by devising a lower-technology challenge for us!"

Rebecca had such a look of pride at having, as she thought, answered the question that I was reluctant to push too hard. "So," I suggested, "a spring isn't doing without technology, but with less of it, right?"

"Yes—but in a positive, creative way. Like, even your example of throwing out your microwave. If you did it hastily, thoughtlessly, then it's just dumb. But if you sat down and made a plan of doing without it—say it included not buying any more frozen dinners and planning to cook your vegetables—then that could be a spring: a lower-technology challenge you've set for yourself."

"And if you had talked me into this project," I said, "then that would be a spark, from your point of view?"

"Exactly," she said. "I guess you could say both of these words refer to challenges involving lower technology." She tapped her fists lightly on the edge of the table. "A good way to put it. Thank you," she said, looking firmly at me, "for helping clear that up. Next time somebody asks me what a spark is, I'll know what to say."

"You know," I said, "it just occurred to me that my trip to Idaho could maybe be considered a spring. You could say a train is lower-technology travel, right?"

Rebecca smiled, nodding cautiously. "You could say that."

We parted with our usual friendly hug, wishing each other happy trips. It always seemed with Rebecca that there was an understanding between us, a rapport that went beyond anything we had communicated with words.

On my Subway trip back home that evening, the strangest thing happened. I was reflecting on the discussion with Rebecca and what it meant in terms of defining the BHB philosophy when I noticed a young woman seated on the seat in front of me. She was wearing a purple tank top that set off her tan complexion and had long, dark hair that spread loosely over her shoulders. I suppose it was her hair that drew my attention to the flesh at the top of her right arm. On it I spotted a little tattoo, of three small letters. I was just able to make them out: BHB.

This is ridiculous! I thought. I've just come from an interview about BHB, and here is a person who is apparently a member! It did occur to me that, somehow, the idea of tattooing your membership on your body for all to see didn't fit in with what I understood about the BHB tendency toward privacy. I sensed that this woman's membership in BHB might be somewhat superficial.

I felt compelled to follow up on this lead. Fortunately, my Local train pulled into 145th Street where it had to wait for the Express, giving us several minutes of quiet in the stopped and nearly empty car.

I stood up. "Excuse me," I said as I came around from behind and sat on the seat facing her. "I saw the BHB on your shoulder, and. . . I wonder, are you a member?"

She drew back, wary of me as a stranger, and obviously puzzled by my question.

"I'm sorry," I continued. "Those letters," I said, pointing at her arm, "I was wondering what they are for?"

"Oh, this?" She pointed toward her arm, but didn't say anything more, still apprehensive about engaging with a stranger.

"Please forgive me," I said. "I know it sounds stupid of me to ask... but I was really curious about what those letters stand for?"

My apologetic words established rapport, and she opened up. "These letters?" she said angrily. "That *was*"—she emphasized the word—"my boyfriend. Bradford Henry Dickerson. The jerk!"

"Oh my," I said. "What happened?"

Now her tone turned sad. "I thought we had it made. But then there was this job in Yellowstone that he simply *had* to take"— her tone was markedly skeptical—"and anyway, it's a long story." Tears started forming around her eyes. "I thought Brad and I really had it made," she repeated, shaking her head. She looked down hard at the floor.

"Well, I'm so sorry about that," I said. Then I remembered something wasn't right about the name.

"You said his name was..."

"Bradford Henry Dickerson. I used to think it was a really neat name. But he's just a pompous ass!"

I looked carefully at the letters again, and saw that she was right. They were BHD. My imagination had been running away with me. I had too much BHB on the mind.

"Well, I am so sorry," I said. After a pause, I continued. "I suppose you want to take those letters off?

"You bet I do," she said bitterly.

"Well, why...?" I let my question hang.

"I can't afford it. My roommate moved out in April and I need every penny to make the rent. I'm eating nothing but macaroni and chickpeas."

"How much would it cost? To remove them."

"They said $100. Two treatments." Her face was blank. She looked exhausted.

I took out my wallet and extracted a $100 bill. "Here," I said, handing it to her. "You get it done." She looked bewildered at first. Then a little smile started to light up her face.

"You mean it?"

"Yes, yes," I said, urging her. "You are too nice a person to let a little thing like that worry you."

She reached cautiously, took the bill, and then clutched it to her breast. She looked up and stared intensely at me. Before I knew it, she lunged forward and kissed me hard on the lips!

At that moment, the Express train screeched into the station on the other track and jerked to a stop. As I rose to go I looked her in the eyes and said, "Good luck!" I found a seat on the Express, and could see her through the window, sitting in the Local, waving goodbye. I waved back.

It occurred to me, as my train pulled away, that the $100 bill I gave the girl could well have been the one Asher had given me in order to, as he said, encourage somebody else to do something creative.

And then another connection hit me: maybe I had accomplished a spark! Certainly, I was playing a role in helping this girl undo a tattoo, which is an aspect of technology. After all, you need modern steel needles to make a tattoo, although, come to think of it, tattoos are pretty ancient, part of primitive cultures. And also, they have to use technology to remove the tattoo, and maybe it's a very modern technology. But then, when you really analyze it, the end result—a bare arm, the way nature originally intended—meant the girl was becoming more like an original human being. One might say.

I sighed. Whatever else all this BHB/technology/spark-spring business amounted to, it certainly was giving my brain a workout.

It crossed my mind that I could ask Rebecca about this episode next time we met. 'Rebecca, is helping someone remove a tattoo considered a spark?' I could see her smiling in confusion at my question, wanting to say, 'It's complicated,' but knowing I would wag my finger at her.

19

A few nights later, after Niccole came back from her stint at the community, our relationship vaulted onto a new and challenging level.

She was in her usual happy mood after being with the children. I set the bowl of macaroni and cheese that I had prepared on the kitchen table, turned off the stove, and took off my apron.

"So, what's new at 107th Street?" I asked as I sat down.

Niccole gave a little dramatic pause before answering. "They are hand washing their own clothes!"

"What?"

She nodded vigorously in reply.

"You can't be serious," I said. "You mean, they're throwing away their washers?"

"And dryers. Not throwing them away, but not using them—for one month. I asked Horace about this, and he explained that it's a carefully thought-out idea."

"I suppose he said it was a spring?" I asked, a certain weariness entering my tone.

"As a matter of fact, he did use that word. I don't know what it means. Do you?"

"Not exactly," I replied, feeling that my head was filled with enough springs and sparks for the time being.

"As I said, it's just for a month," continued Niccole. "After that, they'll go back to using the machines, and then discuss and try to decide what's left them happier, more fulfilled. Probably, Horace said, they'll wind up with some partial arrangement, with some people doing it by hand, and others using machines." After a pause, she said, "Elle claims it's already prompted her to wear her clothes longer before putting them in the laundry—maybe that's a benefit, isn't it?" I made a cautious shrug.

"In any case, I can tell you the kids loved it! The committee figured out at the beginning that everyone should limit the time they put in, so as not to get bored with this task. We set the time for the children at just 20 minutes. Oh my! Elle and I could hardly tear them away from the washboards!. They just loved scrubbing—they were overdoing it, actually. We had to tell them how too much scrubbing can wear out the clothes."

Later, when we were sitting on the sofa in the living room, reading, I looked up at her and said, "I'm going to miss you when I go on Saturday."

"I'm going to miss you, too." Niccole smiled and gave a stage pout. "Going into the Wild West!" Then, still with humor in her eye, she said, "You *are* going to come back, right?"

"Of course." I cradled her face in my hands. "It's only for 10 days."

We looked into each other's eyes. "I've been thinking," I said. Niccole was carefully silent.

"Well, maybe," I continued, "we should talk about what's going on between us?" Niccole's eyes opened wide. She knew what this was about, and I could see she didn't know what direction it was heading. It was some kind of turning point, but she didn't dare guess whether it was for better or for worse.

"I mean, we've never discussed it, but. . ." More silence. Her eyes continued riveted on mine.

"Okay," I said, "I think we should think seriously about getting married." She smiled brightly. "There, now I've said it."

Niccole continued beaming. There was no confusion or hesitation in her gaze. Her head was making tiny, vigorous nods.

"I take it that means you agree with the idea?"

Still, she didn't speak. She just put her arms tightly around me and squeezed very hard.

"Let the record show"—I stepped back and swept my arm out—"that Miss Evenson has agreed with the proposition."

"Oh silly, silly you!"

After several minutes of hugging, we calmed down. "There is one point we should include in our thinking," Niccole said, with a serious tone. "I'm really attracted to the community and the idea of being with children. I'm hoping that will fit in with our plans?"

"Soooo....?"

"Well, I guess it's two points, actually. First, it's children. Are we going to have them?" She looked at me calmly.

"Well, er. . ." I'd been thinking about this issue for many weeks of course, and the more I thought about it, and Niccole's obvious, and natural, attraction to children, the more it seemed that kids were likely to be involved. But I still had the image of myself as the footloose famous novelist, and couldn't turn my back on this model that easily. "It's certainly something to think about. But maybe not right away?"

"Of course, not right away," Niccole said. "We have years to figure things out." This, I thought, is an incredibly wise woman!

Whenever she decides to do something, it will be balanced and thoughtful.

After a few moments, I said, "So what's the second?"

"The second? Oh, yes." She paused. "It's about the community." Her brow furrowed.

"And. . . ?"

"Well, it's important to me. . . ." She let the point hang. When I didn't say anything, she continued, speaking firmly, "I don't want to break my relationship with it."

"Well," I said slowly, "I don't see why you would have to. . .?"

"Because. . . it may get into where we live, eventually?" She paused.

"So you want us to move into 107th Street?"

"Not that exactly, or only. . . ." She looked enquiringly at me.

"But somehow, eventually, couldn't something like that fit into our plans?" After a pause, she continued, "What I'm really, really interested in is this New Hampshire idea." She looked at me intently.

Her declaration exposed the fact that a gap had been developing between us about the philosophy of BHB and the manual community. Niccole, beginning with her attending the Nanoelectronics group, and now working with the children at the community, had rather fully embraced the skepticism of technology that these people seemed to advocate. I felt I was much more of an observer. For me, they were like a new church down the street. She had become a true believer. I was an outsider, merely curious about them. I was ready to write a newspaper article, and even a book, about them, but the idea of signing up and joining was beyond my conception. I wasn't ready for a life-altering conversion, giving up my computer, my phone, my washing machine. And the idea of spending the rest of my life on a farm in New Hampshire seemed quite out of the question.

A wave of deep doubt swept over me. Niccole was such a wonderful woman, and we got along so well, but it was starting to look like we might have incompatible lifestyle preferences.

"Well. . ." I said slowly.

"We don't have to decide now," she said. "You haven't even visited the place and met the people. I'm sure you would like Horace."

I probably would, I thought, but would I want to live the primitive lifestyle he advocated?

"Well, I guess the next thing to do," I said, "is to find out exactly what this New Hampshire thing involves. How many people are there, what does it cost, what rules does it have? Where do you charge your cell phone?" Niccole gave me a stage frown.

"And especially, what kind of commitment do they expect? Are we supposed to live in caves, cold and hungry for the rest of our lives?"

Niccole smiled at my overdramatizing. She assumed I was jesting, but I wasn't sure I was.

20

Niccole came with me to Penn Station on Saturday evening, to launch me on my expedition to the sprawling American continent. It was a night train to Chicago, leaving at 9:40 p.m. There, I would change for the next leg, taking the train known as the Empire Builder, which glided across the next 2,000 miles of the Northwest.

We walked along the platform, past posters tacked up on the wall, one advertising wine, another, an elegant designer dress, and stopped at my car. As I turned to board, Niccole became rather tense.

"Now, you will be careful," she said, grasping my arm.

"Trains don't crash, dear."

"But, as I've said, this seems so strange. I mean, what exactly are you going for and who are you hoping to meet?"

Smiling, I drew into a formal stance. "I am going to meet, and interview, the man who is the head of BHB!" I fist-pumped my chest.

She was not impressed with my play-acting.

"As you know," I continued in a more serious tone, "I am going to write a book about this organization. A book that will make me famous," I added, "and earn a lot of money so we can get married and live happily ever after."

My confident words didn't allay her anxiety. "And if you don't come back, if something happens, who would I contact in what's-its-name, Idaho?"

"Bonners Ferry, a little town in the scenic Rocky Mountains."

"It's such a funny name," she said, still skeptical. "What should anyone need a ferry in the middle of the Rocky Mountains?"

"Actually, I have no idea. I will find out and report back to you!" I gave a tiny salute, and was glad to see her crack a smile. I made a mental note to find out the origin of the town's name. It would be one of those details that would flesh out the description of the BHB headquarters in my book.

"And the man's name?"

"Charles Stephenson."

"Let me write that down. At least I'll have a name."

After she put her notebook away, we hugged again. "Darling, I'll be fine. There's nothing to worry about."

I didn't tell her that I had no street address for Stephenson, just a mail box number. This had worried me at first, the fact that I couldn't directly walk up to the BHB building when I reached Bonners Ferry. But then, as I thought more about it, I figured that in a small town, everyone knows everyone. Once I got there, I would just ask people, and they could tell me where Stephenson lived, or at least where the BHB headquarters building was.

The conductor's whistle blew. I climbed up the steps into the car lugging my suitcase behind.

I had forgotten how large and spacious a train is compared to an airplane. I glanced down the aisle of the nearly empty car, admiring the high ceiling, the chrome trim, and the reclining seats in brown leatherette. Each chair seemed almost wide enough to hold two people. And, of course, the windows were marvelous. On a plane, you have those tiny portholes that you can barely peek out of. Here, giant picture windows ran along both sides of the car. I envisioned myself reclining on my lounge chair with a glass of wine in one hand, looking out on a panoramic vista of sweeping prairie and grazing buffalo.

The emptiness of the car added to the feeling of luxury, making it almost seem like a private car. I had read somewhere that Amtrak needed a huge subsidy to cover its costs. I think the figure I saw was that each passenger on a cross-country trip costs taxpayers something like $4,000. I had paid only $502 for my round-trip ticket. I couldn't decide whether to feel honored, or guilty.

The first leg of the trip passed uneventfully. I tried to sleep, tried to read, visited the lounge for a snack, and watched an episode of *Inspector Mapple* on my phone. In recent weeks, I had been developing a certain hesitation about using the phone—a sensitivity that obviously had something to do with Niccole's radical rejection of the device. Apparently, I was now seeing the world somewhat through her eyes. On this trip, I found that the phone wasn't serving very well as a source of entertainment for me. I would scan headlines on the phone, for example, but found them empty, a puzzling chatter about a distant civilization.

After a night and a day of travel, I got off the train the following evening in Chicago. There I transferred to the Empire Builder. Getting settled in my car, I met a mother and her three children who were also getting on. She was wrestling a large tan suitcase along the aisle and when she reached me, she nodded at it and asked, "Could I ask you a very big favor?"

"Of course," I stood up and hoisted the suitcase into the luggage rack above.

We had the section of the car to ourselves, and they took the seats next to me on the other side of the aisle. Once the train got underway, I observed them more closely. There were two girls, and a little boy who seemed to be about 5 years old. They were very excited, pointing out the window, asking questions about this and that, which the mother patiently answered. After some time, the chattering subsided and the girls took up books. The little boy remained active, wandering up and down the aisle of the car. He had a cute mop of curly blond hair that looked like it had not been combed since birth. When I next noticed him, he had ducked into an empty seat three rows away and was making a little finger-shooting motion at me. I took up the game, and did a stage collapse back sideways, as if hit by a bullet, which made him giggle. Then, I came alive and alert, peeked my head around the edge of the seat, pointed my finger at him, and said, "Bang!" He imitated my hit-by-a-bullet playacting with a dramatic collapse into the seat.

"What are you two doing?" said the mother, laughing. "I hope he's not bothering you."

I leaned over to her. "We're conducting World War Three."

"Well, thank you for entertaining Todd," she said. "He's quite a live wire, as you can see."

"Where are you folks headed?"

"Williston, North Dakota," she replied. "We're moving to live with their grandmother."

"Oh my, that sounds like quite a change, new schools and all."

"Well, that part of it won't be a change because we're

homeschooled." She gave the girls who were reading their books an affectionate glance. After a pause, she continued, "In fact, it's because of homeschooling that we have to move."

"Oh, really? What happened?"

"Well, I don't know if you know this, but school districts give homeschoolers a hard time. There's no end of requirements they keep coming up with." She was speaking energetically now. "The shame of it is we're forced to pay taxes to support them, and then they use the money to harass us."

This was all unknown territory to me. I'd heard of homeschooling, of course, but I assumed it was extremely rare. I never thought I would actually encounter it.

"Their latest thing, what's forcing us to move, is a requirement that the parent has to be credentialed as a tutor! They want me," she pointed her finger at her chest, "to take their silly education courses. They don't seem to care that my girls are two years ahead of their grade level."

"Really?"

"Nadia is 10 and she's doing 7th grade curriculum, and Zoe is 9 and doing 6th grade level."

"Well, that's wonderful," I said, smiling at the girls, who had looked up from their books.

As the trip continued, I visited with Julia, which was the mother's name, and learned about the family's background. Julia's husband was, for the time being, to remain at his job in Naperville, Illinois. He worked for a heating and air conditioning company. "He'll come to Williston for visits, of course," Julia said.

The following afternoon, the train made it to Williston. I carried their tan suitcase down the aisle and out onto the platform, where I wished them all good-bye. "Well, I'm sorry you have to go through this difficult adjustment," I said to Julia. "Breaking up the family and all."

"Oh, it won't be so bad," said Julia, smiling. "We'll figure it out. As Harvey said, we should consider this a spring."

It was like a light bulb popping on, but we were shaking hands at that moment, so it was not the time to follow up on her use of that significant word. All I could do was wave good-bye to the girls, give the brightly smiling Todd a formal handshake—I was starting to feel fond of this special kid—and climb back up into the car.

As the train gathered speed, sliding across the brown prairie in the late afternoon sunshine, I couldn't put from my mind the idea that I had bumped into yet another BHB connection. In just one more day, I thought, all this shadowy ambiguity will be cleared up.

21

Not surprisingly, I was the only passenger getting off the train at Bonners Ferry at 12:45 a.m. (the train was running late—which, as locals later informed me, it usually does). The door on my car was the only one on the entire train that had been opened, and I was the only person getting off. Just seconds after I stepped down, the train began creeping forward again. The conductor quickly grabbed the metal step-stool he had placed on the platform for me to disembark, and swung himself back into the car. He turned in the doorway and gave me a knowing smile, which seemed to say, 'Anyone who's crazy enough to get off here must know what they're doing.'

The noise of the disappearing train soon faded into the darkness. I stood for a moment rocking back and forth on my toes and heels, enjoying the feeling of solid ground under my feet after so many hours riding in the trembling train car. I took a deep breath of the cool night air and contemplated my course of action. There was not a single person along the concrete platform that served as the town's railroad station, or anywhere else in sight. All I could see were streetlights shining through trees along quiet streets, and lights of an occasional car passing along what looked like a main road some blocks away. I pulled out my phone and entered the Ruby Motel. I knew Niccole would disapprove of this reliance on technology, saying that I should ask someone, but there was no one to ask, and I wasn't about to wander around Bonners Ferry, Idaho in aimless circles for the rest of the night. I followed the phone's route to the motel, which was a good half-mile away, greeted the night clerk—a bored young man who could scarcely take his eye off the computer, and accepted the key to my room.

The next morning, refreshed by sleep and a shower, my hair brushed neat, I came into the lobby and approached the desk, primed to ask my critical question. I had relived this moment in my mind's eye many times, the moment of asking where Charles Stephenson lives and getting a bright smile of recognition and careful directions to his house.

A heavy-set older woman with long brown hair was seated behind the counter. She gave me a warm smile of greeting.

"I'm hoping you can help me," I said. "I'm here to find Charles Stephenson, who lives here in Bonners Ferry. I've come a long way to meet him, but I don't know where he lives. Maybe you know him, or there's a local directory where you can look him up?"

There was no smile of recognition, just a blank look. "I don't recognize the name. Let's see," she said, tapping on the computer. Her face grew increasingly worried as she clicked and scanned. "I don't see anything," she said slowly. "Let me ask my manager."

She went into an office in back. After a minute, she came out, trailed by an older man wearing a tan blazer.

"I don't know what to tell you," he said. "Louise says she tried the telephone directory, and he's not in there. Possibly, you could go to the city office, and they could find him from his water bill or tax record—although I doubt they're allowed to give that information out."

"Ohhhh," I said, trying to suppress the wailing tone in my voice. Then I remembered that I had another lead. "Do you know anything about an organization here in town called BHB?" To overcome their blank stares I added, "Being Human Being."

They looked at each other with puzzled frowns and then shook their heads. I could see they were beginning to regard me with a degree of wariness, as if I might have some kind of mental problem. I quickly thanked them and made my way back to my room.

At first, I couldn't accept what was happening to me. I kept shaking my head. This can't be, I thought. I've spent three days and $502 dollars traveling to meet a man who, who. . . doesn't exist! How is this possible?

Gradually, the blunt fact of my gigantic error began sinking in. How had I talked myself into believing that I would arrive in Bonners Ferry and simply walk up to the head of BHB? I suppose it was the fact of having that name, Charles Stephenson, that gave my assumption its feeling of reality. If someone had told me there was "a person" in Bonners Ferry who headed the BHB organization I would have been skeptical, and open-minded about it. I would have done some more research before I left New York. I would have made some phone calls, utilized the Internet.

"You. Are. A. Really. Stupid. Person." I said it out loud several times, as I paced around the room, picking up items and throwing them back down. It occurred to me that, if my father ever found out about this colossal mistake, he would nod with an 'I told you so' grimace.

I walked out of the motel in a glum daze, looking for some way to kill time and push the pain of this stupid error away. With nothing else to do, I walked up the street to the central part of town, glancing at a tire store, a Mexican restaurant, a bookstore. My wanderings took me out along the road leading from town to a long bridge that spanned a surprisingly wide river. I stopped in the middle of the bridge and gazed idly up the wide valley. It was a fine day, a few puffy clouds standing out in the bright blue sky, purple mountains in the distance. As I later learned, I was standing above the Kootenai River, a main tributary of the Columbia River. In olden days, long before the bridge was built, a Mr. Bonner set up a ferry across this river, and that's how this place got its name.

After staring down at the swirling surface of the river for long moments, I returned to the main part of town where I noticed a store called "Under the Sun." This offbeat name roused my curiosity and I went in. I was met by the engaging smell of lavender and the sight of glittering, colorful scarves and shawls hanging from the ceiling. It was a gift shop selling arts and crafts. Spread out along its tables and shelves was a great jumble of herbal lotions and potions, embroidered tea towels, ceramics of all kinds—cups, bowls, highly decorated plates. There was a set of circus figurines, each statuette about five inches high, including a lion tamer with a whip, a juggler with a ball in each hand, and a girl in a silver bathing suit doing a cartwheel.

As I lifted my gaze to take in this vast array of colorful craft creations, the meaning of the store's name finally dawned on me: gathered here, you could say, was everything under the sun.

Among the many handiworks and accessories, the store had

a vast assortment of colorful greeting cards—birthday cards, anniversary cards, get well soon cards. And picture postcards, showing stunning photos of cliffs, mountains and waterfalls. It occurred to me that at least one constructive thing I could do with my time in this town was to send Niccole a card from Bonners Ferry, Idaho. I selected one with a gorgeous panoramic view of the nearby mountains, and, using the counter beside the rack to write on, I jotted her address on it. I was stumped at first about what message to write. "Having a wonderful time!" would have been a lie. "Wish you were here" didn't seem right: it didn't make sense to think of inviting Niccole to join me in my frustrating disappointment. I looked again at the picture on the front and wrote, "You lift me over mountains, Love Jon."

Chatting with the elderly proprietress of the store—it turned out she actually made some of the scented soaps for sale—I got directions to the local post office so I could personally ensure that the card got into the mail. It was only a block away.

As I approached the building with its big American flag out in front, a little bell started ringing at the back of my mind. The one thing I knew about this supposed Charles Stephenson was a post office box number, Box 71. Of course, that might be fictitious, too, I realized. There might be no Box 71, or, if there was, it might have nothing to do with any person I was interested in. But still, I thought, it was a detail I might as well look into.

I went up the granite steps into the building, pushed through the main door, and went to the window where I bought my stamp: one post card stamp, undoubtedly the smallest sale that the clerk had made all year. I dropped the card in the outgoing mail slot. It occurred to me that I might beat it back to New York City. Then

I went over to the section with the mailboxes on the left side of the main lobby. They were numbered consecutively, so there had to be a Box 71. I noticed, as I ran my eye along the wall, that each mailbox had a little glass window in front—I guess so customers could see if they had mail. I came to Box 71. I bent down and peered at the little window. There was a letter in it! I put my eye to the glass and inspected the address on the letter. Fortunately, the letter was right side up, and I could just make out the name. It was not Charles Stephenson. Peering and refocusing several times, I determined that the name was Wayne Davis!

Could this be the real name of the man I was seeking? Having been fooled once, I told myself, I had better be skeptical and cautious. But still, I could not resist a rising sense of excitement.

I hurried back to the Ruby and pushed through the lobby door. The lady at the desk gave a cautious smile at my eagerness. "How about the name 'Wayne Davis'?" I asked.

"Oh, I know him," she said. She seemed relieved to learn that I was a normal person who knew the names of real people. "He and his wife are realtors. I seem to remember he was president of the Rotary. Let me get his address from the town directory." She typed into the computer. "He lives at 606 Myrtle Creek Drive. That's just up on the hill behind here," she said, pointing over her shoulder.

"Thank you, thank you, so much!" I said, letting out a great breath of relief. "Wayne Davis 606 Myrtle Creek Drive." I repeated it to anchor it in my memory.

In less than 10 minutes I had walked up a rather steep, winding street to a big white house with green-trimmed windows. It had a wide, roofed-over front porch where two green lawn chairs stood beside a metal table with several books on it.

I approached the door, took a deep breath, and pressed the button. I could hear it ringing inside.

After what seemed like a long time, the door was swung open by an older man with thinning gray hair. He was wearing a blue work shirt that flopped down over his jeans.

"Yes?" he said.

"Excuse me," I said, "but I'm looking for Wayne Davis."

"Well, you have found him. What can I do for you?" My heart jumped. Was I, at long last, successful in finding the human being in charge of the BHB?

I knew I had to proceed carefully and politely. "I'm so glad to meet you," I said. "My name is Jon Jones, and I've come from New York. By train, actually."

"My goodness!" he said.

"Well, I hope you'll forgive me, but I'm following up on a document—a very excellent, thought-provoking document"—I hoped flattery might help break the ice—"that you may have written. It was titled 'Humility.'"

The man's face instantly lost its look of apprehension. "Oh that!" he said, smiling broadly. "How on earth did you ever find out about that?" Then, before I could begin to answer, he stepped back from the door. "Come in, come in!"

I followed him into the living room, thrilled to know that I had finally reached my objective. "Sit down," he said, indicating an armchair. "Now, go on," he said. "What can I tell you?"

"Well, to begin with, are you the author of that 'Humility' paper?"

"Yes, I am," he said. "Or at least a paper with that title."

Score one for the intrepid reporter! I thought to myself, although I was a little puzzled by the tone of his answer. He was not proud, as I would have expected, but rather guarded.

"Well, I'd just like to understand more about BHB, an organization which I gather you are in charge of?"

"I beg your pardon?" he said. "I don't know. . . . What is this B. . . thing?"

"BHB," I said. "It's at the bottom of your paper. Right on the page."

"Really? On the page?" he said. "You say it says BHB? That's curious." He gave a frown. "Let me go get it so we know what we're talking about."

He rose and went into the adjacent room, which I gathered was his office. I heard a filing cabinet open. After a minute, he came back with a paper in his hand. "Is this what we're talking about?" He handed it to me.

I looked at it carefully. The title was the same, "Humility." I scanned the sentences, and all of the wording seemed the same as I remembered. But then I saw, at the bottom, not the capital letters BHB. They were the letters BFI. This was deeply puzzling.

"What does this 'BFI' mean?" I asked.

"Bonners Ferry, Idaho," he said.

"And why. . . ?" He grimaced, looked sideways toward the window, then looked back at me. "It's complicated."

My heart sank on hearing these familiar words. He went on, "I thought there had to be something at the bottom, some indication of source. Well, I wasn't about to put my name, or even my initials. So, I put this abbreviation of my location." He paused, frowning. "I'm sorry. I realize it does seem a little strange."

"So why not put your name down at the bottom?" I asked.

"Yes, yes, how to explain that?" he said, speaking to himself, looking at the ceiling. He took a deep breath.

"At the time I wrote that, I still had hopes of getting another academic position. You see, I had just left—or rather, been forced to leave—the University of Colorado. I was an associate professor in linguistics. Well, if you know anything about academia, you know that they resist original ideas, unusual ideas. That's why I was being pushed out of UC. I had given a paper about the questionable status of deconstructionism and my colleagues, shall we say, took umbrage. Well, I didn't want any more black marks on my resume. I couldn't have my name associated with anything as iconoclastic as that statement." He indicated the paper in my hand.

"And that's why you used a pseudonym when you sent it to Professor Mark Thurlow?"

"Right," he said, in a tone of resignation. "My goodness, you've really done your research!" he nodded toward me with a smile. Then he continued, "I told Mark in my cover letter that we had been together in graduate school—which was true—and hoped he would assume the pseudonym was simply someone he didn't remember."

There was a pause. I felt dazed, disoriented. "And what about the other BHB documents? Did you write those?"

"What other documents?"

"Like the one with the title 'The Power of Boredom.' Did you write that?"

"I don't. . . I don't recognize it."

My brow furrowed. "So you've never heard of BHB?" I asked.

He shook his head. "What does it mean?"

At first, I ignored his question, lost in my disappointment. I took a deep breath, looked at the ceiling, then out the window. Finally, I registered his question and looked back at him and said, without expression, "Being human being."

He perked up. "That's interesting! So, what's the philosophy of this organization?"

"Well, that's what I'm trying to establish. At the center of it, I guess, is questioning technology, arguing that it can take away from human happiness and fulfillment."

"Boy, you can say that again! Hey, where do I sign up?"

A little cry of despair escaped my lips. I had travelled three days and 2,400 miles to locate the top official in the BHB organization. Now that I had—after some quite clever and persistent sleuthing—located this man, it turns out that he knows nothing about this organization, and he wants *me* to tell *him* how to become a member! The irony of his question was all too painful.

My expression of deep dismay concerned him. "Are you okay?" he asked.

I stared at the carpet, unable to think what to do next. "Yea, I guess so," I said slowly.

He jumped up from his chair. "Here, let me get you something. Coffee, soda, water?"

"A little water would be fine."

After he set the glass on the table he asked, "So, are you a reporter, or something? Writing a book about this BHB organization?"

"Well, a freelance reporter. And yes, I was hoping to write a book about BHB. But I find it is very shadowy, very adverse to publicity!"

"That's it!" said Wayne excitedly. "That's what it should be."

"Now wait a minute," I said. "You said you didn't know anything about it."

"I don't. But you said it was a technology-questioning group. And being averse to publicity is, in my opinion, a bedrock issue when it comes to questioning technology—like I said in my 'Humility' essay."

"I guess I don't understand," I said.

"It goes back to language and communication. These are technological advances. Yes, they have benefits, but they also have dangers."

"The biggest danger," he went on, "is they allow humans to organize themselves into extremely large units, like nations and empires, and let them suppose that these units can be wisely and productively directed—which they can't be."

"Uuuhhh," was all I could say. I was feeling so drained by the let-down over BHB that I couldn't really follow what Wayne was saying. I was still trying to get my mind around the contradiction I had stumbled into. On the one hand, people talked about belonging to BHB, and being led by its ideas, but, on the other, it was not an organization, and it did not seem to have, as I had just so painfully discovered, any leader.

"But listen," Wayne was saying, "I can see you've had a hard trip and probably need some rest."

"Yes, I think I could use a nap," I said as I got up to go.

At the door, Wayne made a suggestion. "Listen, if you're free tomorrow, you might be interested in going huckleberry picking with us. My wife and I are going. It would give you a chance to get outdoors. Hey," he said with a broad smile, "we couldn't let a tourist from New York City come here and not see our mountains."

I agreed to come back to the house on the morrow, dressed, as he advised, in my most casual clothes—especially a long-sleeved shirt to protect my arms—and be introduced to the Roman Nose huckleberry fields.

I walked slowly down Myrtle Creek Drive back to my motel. My dominant thought was disappointment, of course. Disappointment at not finding what I set out to find. But as I kicked the pebbles on my path, the feeling began to grow that perhaps I had also uncovered something positive. Wayne's remarkable awareness of the BHB thrust seemed to suggest the existence of a larger reality lying beyond formal organizations. This man, living on the other side of the country, had independently arrived at the technology-questioning ideas emerging in New York.

It was like finding a single piece of a jigsaw puzzle on the street. That little piece of distinctively-shaped wood isn't an answer to anything. But it tells you that there is a larger picture, somewhere.

22

"Well, it is true that bears like huckleberries. In fact, it's their main food, I think."

This was the reply that Alice, Wayne's wife, gave me when I asked her about the danger of bears as we were driving up the long dirt road to the mountain called Roman Nose. I had remembered that Rebecca mentioned bears in connection with her Catskill Mountain outing.

"But you don't have to worry about them," Wayne said. "Really. People from the cities don't seem to understand this, but humans are not the bear's natural prey. Bears are shy. They run away from you."

"That's right," said Alice. "The two times I've seen a bear, they were moving away each time."

Alice had been a ski instructor in Colorado when she met Wayne. They had lived for many years in Boulder, home of the University of Colorado. They moved to Bonners Ferry when Wayne quit his job there, and together they ran a real estate business in the area. Alice was a short, slender woman with an attractive bob of platinum blond hair. Maybe it was gray, but it still looked good.

As the winding road rose higher, the spectacular vista broadened until we could see scores of miles across the valley to other mountain ranges. Huckleberries, Wayne said, only grow

161

at higher elevations, above about 4,000 feet. That means that picking them is a major outing into the mountains. The serious, commercial pickers come and stay for days, camping next to the fields. We passed several of their parked campers on our way up.

Finally, Wayne said, "Let's try here," and pulled to the side of a wide spot and parked. We got out, made our way through the brush at the edge of the road onto steeply-sloping open land, and sure enough, there were the huckleberries. Not that they were easy to pick. For one thing, the bushes, which are 3 to 4 feet high, don't grow together in a mass, like blackberries. They stand separately, scattered here and there. And the berries themselves do not grow in clumps that you can strip in a handful with one pull. They grow individually at the end of tiny stems, so you have to pick each one—which is tiny, about the size of a pea—one at a time. Since each bush has only about 10 to 15 berries, you have to keep moving, pushing through undergrowth, climbing over dead logs, to the next one. There is no resting.

I found the activity strangely intoxicating, however. It becomes rather like an addiction that you can't stop. There's always that one more berry to pick. It crossed my mind that maybe humans are somehow programmed to pick berries the way birds are programmed to peck for insects.

Because the berries are so thinly spaced, pickers tend to spread out, so we were soon dispersed over the hillside, often out of sight of each other. So, there was little possibility of conversation. Each picker is a lonely bird, following its instinct. But, as I said, the task is strangely satisfying. When the time came to pack up, I found myself reluctant to go. In making my way back to the car, I repeatedly stopped to pick a few more berries.

"It's hard to quit, isn't it, Jon?" Wayne said, as I approached the car.

In the car on the way down, Alice made a suggestion. "If you'd like, Jon, I can make your berries into jam for you to take back to New York. Huckleberries don't keep very long after they're picked."

"Yes," Wayne said. "Unlike most other berries, they don't separate cleanly at the stem when you pick them. Each berry is partly torn open. That's why your fingers are all stained."

He was certainly right about that. My fingers were purple! (and the stain, I learned, didn't wash off for several days).

The berry expedition was repeated the following day, at a different mountain south of town. Again, we had a spectacular vista of mountains and cliffs. One point I especially noticed was that all of the pine trees—well, conifers, as Wayne taught me to say, since they include larches, firs, and spruces—were so narrow and tall. They were like spires that turned the mountainsides into a cathedral.

I was pleased to see my competence as a picker had improved; in about the same amount of time that afternoon, I picked almost twice as many berries. I think I was learning to spot from a distance which bushes were more heavily-bearing. When we made it back to town, Alice took my pail of berries, and promised to have the jam ready that evening, when I was invited to their home for supper.

At the motel, I packed my bag and made final arrangements at the desk, for I was to get on board the train and head home late that night.

Later, I made my way back up Myrtle Creek Drive, enjoying

the late afternoon sunlight. I had been quite surprised to find how much longer the summer days were here compared to New York City because it's so far north. Before I came, I hadn't realized that the top part of Idaho, where Bonners Ferry is, lies farther north than the tip of Maine.

Alice had prepared a scrumptious dish of lasagna to feed the appetite I had built up scrambling up and down the mountain slopes in pursuit of huckleberries. In praising it I said, "You must be Italian!"

She smiled. "Well, I had an Italian boyfriend once." She exchanged a knowing glance with Wayne.

I had resolved to use the occasion of this going-away meal to see if I could make some headway in unravelling the BHB business. That Wayne wasn't a part of it, I now fully accepted. But it did appear he had an understanding of the social issues that were bound up in this organization. After we had finished dessert—huckleberry ice cream, of course! —I explained to Wayne and Alice the background of my trip.

"It's been my object to write a book about this BHB organization. Given what everybody's saying about the evils of technology, it could be a very popular book." I gave a little shrug. "Even a bestseller." Wayne and Alice smiled politely.

"But what I don't understand," I continued, "and what I'm trying to research, is why this organization is so secretive, so afraid of being in the limelight."

Wayne and Alice looked at me with interest.

"I'm convinced," I went on, "that the BHB people have no violent or harmful purpose in mind. So why do they shun publicity? Do you have any idea?"

Wayne nodded thoughtfully at my question. "I think there may be more to this BHB group than you realize." He leaned back.

"Publicity is the life blood of large groups. All this impressive stuff—bigness and publicity and fame—is the result of technology: printing, newspapers, electronic amplifiers. What happens is humans become overloaded with facts and opinions, much faster than they can digest.

"All this technology makes it possible for leaders like a Hitler to reach into the minds of tens of thousands. The result is that instead of each person thinking for himself, weighing what his neighbor says, thoughtfully reaching conclusions, people become tools of mass movements and demagogues—and that leads to ruin!"

"Dear. . . ." Alice said gently, laying a hand on his wrist. I noticed she was wearing a delicate silver bracelet with a little heart on it.

"Sorry, sorry," Wayne said to me. "I sometimes get a little carried away."

"No," I replied. "Don't apologize. I'm just having a hard time getting my mind around what you're saying. I. . ." I paused. "You're saying we should keep fame and publicity out of deciding about how we should live. . . ?"

"Now," Alice said gently, "that's enough philosophy for tonight, gentlemen. I wanted to ask," she said turning to me, "Jon, are you married?"

I understood that she saw her role, after being a professor's wife for many years, as one of keeping conversations from getting too controversial.

"As a matter of fact," I replied, "I'm right on the verge of getting married. I've just proposed to my girlfriend, and. . . she has, sort of, accepted. Now. . . we're deciding whether we can make it work."

"What's her name?"

"Niccole."

"Oh, what a nice name," said Alice. "What seems to be standing in the way?"

"Well. . ." I didn't know quite how to begin. "Actually"—I gave a little laugh—"it's about technology." I winked and tipped my head toward Wayne. "I'm sorry to go back to the same old topic."

Alice smiled. "What do you mean?"

"Well, Niccole, who is a really special, wonderful woman"—I nodded to emphasize the point—"is rather opposed to relying on electronic things, and—it's a long story—but anyway, she wants to live a rather primitive lifestyle, one that emphasizes manual labor."

"Well, good for her! I say," said Wayne.

"Wayne, dear," said Alice, nodding in his direction, "let him finish."

"I do sort of admire her for it," I said, acknowledging Wayne's comment. "But the problem is, I don't know whether I can be comfortable matching her level of abstinence."

Then I added, jokingly, "It's hard to give up CanyaCong." Alice and Wayne looked at each other. I suspected they had a lot to say but, out of politeness, didn't want to seem to criticize me or give advice.

"Oh, I'm sure you'll find a way," Alice said, giving a reassuring nod.

After we had finished supper, Alice went into the kitchen and came back with a compact cardboard box that contained six little sealed jars of huckleberry jam.

"This is for you—and Niccole."

I lifted one of the gleaming jars and inspected the dark purple jam. "Thank you so much. I know she'll love these, especially when I tell her it was my own manual labor that picked the berries."

Alice gave a knowing smile. "Well, I wish you two all the best." She turned to Wayne, "I think we can recommend the institution of marriage, can't we?"

"Yes," he said, looking at her with a smile. Then he said to me, "But I'm not planning to go on television about it."

We all laughed.

23

Much later that evening I boarded the Empire Builder for my long trip back to New York.

I was in a mood of exhilaration—which was a bit puzzling. After all, I had not been successful in finding an official headquarters of BHB, and the man who I thought was supposed to be the head of this organization had nothing to do with it. So, in a formal sense, my trip had been a failure. And the idea of writing a book about BHB seemed further away than ever.

However, despite this failure, the trip felt rewarding, energizing. I had gotten to know a very interesting couple, and through them gained a certain insight about BHB that I certainly never expected. I also experienced quite an outdoor adventure. The huckleberry picking was a manual task that I found surprisingly fulfilling.

As the train wound its way among the mountains, I dozed, read some, and watched the fields sliding by in the nighttime. My mind was focused on the phone call I was planning to make to Niccole. It was Friday and, allowing for the time difference, she would be receiving calls starting at 4:00 a.m. my time. The moment came quickly. I was eager to tell her about my trip and report that I was heading back to her.

We were halfway across Montana when the hour came. She answered on the first ring.

"Oh, I'm so glad to hear your voice!" she said with excitement and relief in her voice. "I've been so worried about you!"

I was touched that I was so important to her.

"Oh, I've been fine." I was tempted to make a wisecrack about escaping grizzly bears, but decided she might take it too seriously. "This is wonderful country out here," I continued. "Someday you must come with me here. Really amazing mountains!"

I went on to tell her I was bringing six jars of huckleberry jam. "And I picked the huckleberries myself," I said proudly.

I didn't see the point of trying to explain the disappointment of not finding the BHB headquarters, and what this might mean for my proposed book. "How are things going at the community?"

"Oh, wonderful! I so much like to be there!" She paused, aware of having raised the sensitive point about whether I would be able to adopt this lifestyle if we got married. "Horace says he's looking forward to meeting with you when you get back," she went on. "I'm sure he'll explain everything to you."

Niccole's mentioning this appointment brought home to me that this meeting could be far more important for my book project than I had assumed. Now that I knew there was no BHB in Bonners Ferry, Idaho, it appeared that Horace and his manual community on 107th Street might be the closest thing to a headquarters for the BHB organization that I was going to get. At least, I could hope, he would be some kind of institutional leader for me to feature in my account of the organization.

"Yes," I said, "tell him I'm looking forward to seeing him, too. Definitely." After wishing each other love, we reluctantly hung up.

The journey home continued with the quiet, undramatic feel that, I was coming to see, marks long-distance train travel. It's quite unlike an airplane trip, where everything happens urgently, under a tight time schedule, with doors slamming shut just in time and screaming engines eager to leave the ground. A train journey is relaxed; one is almost suspended in time. You can hardly tell when the train begins to move. You sit, read a little, think, visit the observation lounge, and watch the fields and distant mountains beyond the windows.

The unsuccessful result of this long, cross-country expedition brought to mind a little verse attributed to David Norris that I had memorized in seventh grade. As I gazed at the tan landscape sliding by, the lines kept cycling in my head:

I left them to paint a star.
But when I got there,
Everything was light, and light,
And I couldn't tell where the light left off and the star began!
So I came back home and snuggled in with the mortals.

On the last day, as the train was gliding its way across western New York State, the calm passivity of my trip was broken by an exceptional contact. In the morning, after the sun had risen, I left my seat and made my way to the snack bar in the lower level of the next car. Across the table from where I sat with my coffee and cinnamon roll sat an older man with his coffee, looking out the window as the fields slid by. He was nearly bald and was wearing a khaki shirt and matching trousers—obviously traveling gear. A closed book lay on the table in front of him and I could see the title, *The Zealot.*

When the man turned to look at me, I said, pointing at it, "That book looks interesting."

"Oh, it is indeed!" He had what sounded to me like a strong English accent.

"Are you from England?"

"Scotland, actually. Glasgow." He pronounced it something like 'Glahsgaahh.'

"You Yanks keep makin' that mistake," he continued, speaking with a twinkle in his eye. "In point of fact, there be many accents you folks call English. Nae jest Scottish, but Irish, Welch—nae t' mention regional tongues. In Scotland, there be at least three, dependin' on how ye tally 'em." He smiled broadly, "But I've got used ta' it here, bein' accused o' bein' English." He gave a conspiratorial wink.

Taking up his bantering, I said, "Well, please forgive my false accusation!" We smiled and I continued, "So are you here for sightseeing?"

"Aye, indeed!" His eyes lit up. "I've come to the States many a time, but always East on business, especially New York. I at last decided that I owed it to me'self to see the West." He waved his hand at the panorama beyond the window. "And it's been worth it. The vast space, all the. . . the high mountains. It just lifts me spirits!"

We were quiet for a moment. "Ye be asking about this book?" He tapped the cover.

"Yes. So. . . what is it about?"

"Aah!" he said with an eager smile. He picked the paperback up and waved it gently toward me. "It has a highly unusual theory about the Bible and the origin of Christianity."

"Really?" I took a sip of coffee. "So what is this theory?"

He put the book down and looked at me. "Ah! You see, the

usual idea is that there was this man, Jesus, who walked up and down the land of Galilee, and said things, and did things that were written down by observers. These were the people—Matthew, Mark, Luke, and John—who wrote the gospels.

"Well, research has shown that the gospels emerged many decades after the death of Jesus, even more than a hundred years later. T'were no actual observers, no Matthew, no Mark, and such. Instead, what ye had was an oral tradition, where dozens—hundreds—of people passed along their ideas about what they supposed had happened, and what they supposed Jesus had said. Then at some point, all this word-of-mouth material got written down by different recorders, and they took fictitious names—Matthew, Mark, and so on—to create the appearance of eyewitness reporting."

"Hmm. . . you mean, then, that Christianity isn't a specific doctrine created by one person?"

"Right. At least, that's what this author says," he said, tapping the book. "Naturally, this view be making some devout Christians irate, because they want to believe what's in the Bible is exactly what Jesus did and said at a particular moment in time." He picked up the book and looked at it thoughtfully.

"But you *could* say that this idea of the Bible stories emerging later"—he said, waving the book back and forth—"*strengthens* the validity of the points being made in the Bible." I frowned. He paused, savoring my puzzlement.

"Ye could say Christianity tis an organic religion. Isn't simply a factual report o' what one man did and said in Palestine in the year 32 AD. Instead, the Bible contains the aggregate wisdom o' many people who lived in many different places all over the

Roman empire, especially cities like Rome and Athens. It is a distillation o' the thinkin' of hundreds of different activists, grappling with points o' morality and philosophy over a century of time."

After a pause, he added, in a serious tone, "And ye could say that the spirit of God was at work shaping this collective wisdom."

"Wow, that really... is... an interesting idea." Of course, there was no way I could bring him up to speed on my BHB chase. All I could say, as I got up to return to my car, was, "Thank you *very* much for bringing this idea to my attention. By the way, what's your name?"

"Ian. Ian McDade. And you...?"

"I'm Jon Jones." He stood and we shook hands. "Thank you very much," I said. "You've really given me a lot to think about."

"My pleasure," he said. Then he added, looking me in the eye, "May God be with ye." His broad smile suggested these words conveyed multiple levels of meaning. Something gave me the idea that he was a pastor or priest—or at least had been earlier in his life.

My mind raced as I made my way up the tiny spiral stairway to the upper deck and walked along the aisle back to my seat. Could this be what BHB was, an aggregate understanding? Transmitted anonymously over time?

The more I thought about it, the more sense it made. Yes! I had been looking at BHB in too mechanical a fashion, as a structured organization operated by someone to accomplish a specific purpose. Now I was beginning to see it should be considered more like a social tide, a movement comprising multitudes of people moving in the same direction.

Back at my seat, I thought back over my meeting with Wayne in Bonners Ferry. You could say that I had seen him as the 'Jesus' of the BHB movement, the source of its writings and ideas. Clearly, he was not. But he did have something to do with it. A hundred years from now, an historian might call him the founder, and attribute the BHB philosophy to him, just as I had been tempted to do.

But there was no founder, no single mind! BHB thinking and practices were a growing, collective understanding. It is an evolving body of ideas, formed by many people over the years, like the early followers gave rise to Christianity in the Roman empire.

Then it hit me: this organic social movement needed someone to record its collective wisdom. Maybe, I thought, I could be the Matthew of BHB!

24

Two days after I returned to New York, Asher and I sat down for a long, relaxed dinner. We had an enormous amount of catching up to do. A month ago, he had taken his vacation—to visit his elderly mother in Arizona—leaving me to run the office, and, when he returned, I had gone on my trip to Idaho, so we hadn't actually talked with each other for a long time. And the load at the office since we both returned had been hectic, so we hardly had a moment to say hello during work.

The Shamrock Grill was relatively quiet that Wednesday evening, and we found our table in the back, under the big photograph of a basketballer shooting a vigorous layup.

After we had ordered our drinks, I asked, "So, did you get some good hiking in?"

"I sure did," Asher replied. "Phoenix has some great routes nearby. I did Echo Canyon twice, going up Camelback," he said. "You know, I just can't get over the crisp, vivid views you get in that dry, western air. You see these spectacular landscapes 40, 50 miles away. It shows you what a sewer we're in here, with our humidity and pollution. We can't see even 5 miles—on a clear day—in New York."

Of course, I had to share my experience in the Idaho Mountains, and we chatted about Western and Eastern scenery.

"By the way," Asher said, "Why did you pick that place—what was it?"

"Bonners Ferry."

"Yes. What was there for you?"

I leaned back into the leather cushion. "It's a long story."

"Fine," said Asher. "We've got all night. Let's hear it."

"Okay, okay," I said. After a pause, I began, "There's a thing called BHB—I don't suppose you've ever heard of it?"

His reply practically knocked me out of my seat. "Sure I have," he said. "I've been involved with it for years."

I stared at him for many long seconds, my head reeling with the coincidence of this declaration. Here I had been chasing all across the country to find this elusive organization, and now it turns out my boss knew about it all along.

"What's the matter?" Asher asked, puzzled by my silent, riveting gaze.

"It's just that I, I didn't guess. . . ."

"Well, maybe I've never mentioned it to you, but it's important to me. I go to two different exploration groups. I have a lot of friends there." After a pause he went on. "Anyway, now you know. So, what did BHB have to do with your trip?"

"Well," I said slowly, "I've been hoping to write about this organization, and I got the idea that it had, well, some kind of headquarters in Bonners Ferry, Idaho."

"And did it?"

I gave him a sheepish grin and hung my head. "No."

"I'm not surprised," Asher said. "From all that I've seen, BHB doesn't have any kind of formal organization."

"Then what is it?" I asked, with urgency and irritation in my voice.

"That's a good question. It's a kind of—what would be the word?" He paused. "Maybe you could call it an 'organic movement.'

I perked up. There was that word 'organic' again, the same term that Ian on the train used to describe the early evolution of Christianity! "What do you mean?"

"Something that grows out of the earth," Asher said. He saw I was still puzzled. "Okay, let's use an analogy. People hold doors open for each other, right? Where did that practice come from? There's no 'Holding Doors Open Association.' There's no president and board of directors. Holding doors open is just something that grows up organically. People see that it makes sense.

"It's the same way with BHB. People see that you've got to start questioning technology, to explore healthy ways to limit it. I mean, it's obvious. If we just lap up every new thing, we're going to become robots." He paused. "Unhappy robots."

We were back to the Asher I knew, with his idea that phones make people unhappy. Now I saw that this idea of his wasn't just a passing notion, but part of his entire worldview.

"Okay, maybe there's something to that," I said. "But why isn't BHB just an anti-technology group—like environmental groups are against pollution and cancer groups are against cancer? Why doesn't it have a headquarters? And a web site?"

"Ah, that's an interesting point, isn't it?' Asher said, taking off his glasses and setting them down on the table. "One theory is that a mass organization relies on technology: electronics, mass printing, and so on. So, to form such an organization, you would rather have to compromise your ideals."

I looked at him quizzically.

"I mean," continued Asher, "if someone asked me to organize a convention of BHB, I would shy away. It would mean I would be up to my neck in technology to make it happen: computers, e-mails, phones. I'd be uncomfortable about that."

I nodded. It seemed that at last, some of the pieces of the BHB puzzle were starting to come together.

"Another question I have," I said, "is why the organization is so secretive? It's almost like it's a conspiracy. What does it have to hide?"

"Yes," said Asher, slowly, thoughtfully. "Part of it, like I said, is that publicity involves technology, and we shy away from that." He looked up at me. "But there's more, too. Part of it, I think, is this feeling that we simply don't have the answers."

"What do you mean?"

"Well. . ." He paused, then looked up at me. "The world is very complicated. Figuring out the right way to go needs to be a very thoughtful, gradual process. A large, formal organization, almost by definition, has to claim to know the truth. It has to have manifestos, position papers. . . ."

In response to my look of puzzlement, he went on. "That has been the tragedy of human history. Large organizations—political parties, governments—think they know the answers, and end up plunging everybody into ruin."

It seemed to be a pretty big point, bigger than I could quite get my brain around at the moment. I couldn't think of anything to say. We sat quietly for some moments. "Well, anyway," I said, returning to Asher's original question about why I was interested in BHB, "I've been hoping to write about this BHB business, whatever it is, maybe a book or something." It was more of a question than a statement of fact. I was hoping to get his reaction to the viability of such a book.

"That could be interesting," was all he said.

I went on to tell him about my upcoming interview with Horace at the manual community, and the conversation moved on to Niccole and her role there. I told him we were moving toward getting married, and that Niccole wanted us to move into the manual community for a few months, and then to the New Hampshire commune after that. I shared with him my reservation about being able to adopt the manual community's lifestyle.

"But we're really in love!" I went on. "You should have seen us when we got together after my trip to Idaho. She was just bubbling! She had been really worried about me. We couldn't stop holding each other."

Asher smiled indulgently. "Well, I'm sure you'll find a way to work things out." He had a sly grin, as if he knew something about us that I wasn't aware of. I searched my mind. What could he possibly know about my relationship with Niccole that I didn't?

Then it hit me! I drew a deep breath.

"That was a spark!" I said, staring at him. "The challenge you set for me with Niccole back at Thompkins Park, about her not using her phone for a day. That was a spark!"

Asher grinned broadly, enjoying my being flabbergasted.

I thumped my fist on the table. "You set that whole thing up."

He smiled, then gave a tiny shrug that said, 'Could be.'

We silently grinned at each other for a long time. Finally, I said, "Well, I guess I have to thank you." I let out a big breath. "It was a brilliant example of a technology-reducing challenge," I said. "It certainly has made a world of difference in my life! In fact, it has changed my whole life. And Niccole's, too."

Asher basked in my compliment.

"You should tell them about it at your next BHB exploration," I told him.

"I already have," he said, with a twinkle in his eye.

25

"In any case, we would have to live at 107th Street for at least three months before we can go to New Hampshire."

We had just finished supper in our apartment. Niccole had cleared the plates from the table and we sat facing each other, holding hands on top of the red-and-white checkered tablecloth.

"That's their requirement," she continued. "The idea is to give everybody a chance to see if we are really serious about the commitment."

I was to meet with Horace the next afternoon, and Niccole and I had realized that this would be more than an information-collecting interview for my book. It would also be the start of an application process to join the community, and would bring up issues that would affect our future together.

In the days since I had returned from Idaho, it had become increasingly clear that Niccole had set her heart on going to the New Hampshire Farm. She hadn't said that marriage was out of the question if I refused to go. But that was the direction things were heading. For my part, it was becoming increasingly clear that committing to New Hampshire would be a big strain on my lifestyle. I would find out more about this challenge from Horace, but I already knew from Niccole that they were really serious about cutting back on technology. Even at the manual community at 107th Street there was basically no

TV, and no microwave ovens, and I didn't know what else.

"Those three months at 107th Street will give us both a chance to see how we adjust to the manual principles," Niccole was saying.

"Yes, but what if you adjusted fine, and I didn't?"

"Then we would work something out. We're in this together," she said with an intense expression. "I love you!"

After a few moments silence, I said, "And then there's the question of how do we raise children in that environment? Maybe they can't stand it."

"Oh, don't be silly. They'll love it," she said.

"I also found out some more about signing up for the Farm. Their aim is to have about 150 people and they have 138 there now, so there's room for us. And the cost, the initial buy-in, is $2,000 apiece. So, it's a pretty serious commitment."

She looked pleadingly into my eyes. "You know, it wouldn't have to be for our whole lives," she continued. "We can leave any time we want. I asked about that, too."

I appreciated her trying to be accommodating, but I knew there was more to it than that. If it turned out that I couldn't stand hoeing corn and reading Victorian novels in the evenings by kerosene lamplight, and Niccole couldn't live without this kind of thing, we would have to split. It seemed to me that it would be taking a great chance to commit to a marriage given this underlying uncertainty. I definitely needed a clearer picture of what this organization was all about.

The next afternoon, I left work early and made my way to 107th Street to meet with Horace for what seemed likely to be one of the most important interviews of my life. Not only would it affect

Niccole's and my personal plans. It also was central to unraveling the puzzle of BHB so that I could flesh out my book. Right now, this book, which had seemed such a promising way to make my debut as an author, was rather in limbo. There was nothing in Bonners Ferry to write about, and, as Asher had confirmed, no national organization or national headquarters. My hope now was to produce an interesting, inspiring exposé of this manual community and its New Hampshire "farm," and the philosophy they believed in. For this, Horace would be a central source.

From the moment I pushed through the main door and was welcomed by Dani, the hostess on duty, I was impressed by the positive energy of the place. Everyone, it seemed, was engaged in animated, energetic communication. And not just the adults. There were teens in small groups, eagerly conversing. Passing one group, I overheard one boy say, "And a second reason is. . . ."

People seemed unusually friendly, even the smaller children. As we came up to a little boy about seven years old, Dani introduced me: "Nicolas, this is Mr. Jones."

Now, most children in this situation give a brief, shy glance, then duck their heads and rush away. But not here. The little tyke looked me in the eye, extended his hand, gave me a confident shake and said, "Hello, I'm Nicolas. Pleased to meet you." He could have been running for the U.S. Senate.

As we walked along, I heard, coming from behind a closed door, the sound of a trumpet practicing. As we passed, Dani turned to me, "Almost everyone here plays an instrument. We have lots of recitals."

"Do you play?"

"I'm a cellist," she said proudly.

I was especially struck by the artwork mounted all along the walls, a great variety of pieces, works of children's art, and also mature pieces, some abstract and others carefully representational.

"Every three months, everyone has to take everything down," Dani said, "and we have empty walls for one day. Then people start putting things up again—new works."

"Are they for sale?" I asked.

"Oh, yes, indeed," she said. She peered along the corridor. "See here," she said, pointing to a pink card under one painting, "this one's been spoken for." It was a striking painting of a dense forest with an array of vertical tree trunks making an abstract, geometric design. I was almost tempted to write a higher price bid on the pink card.

Dani took me to Harold's office, knocked and opened the door. A man was seated at a long work table on the side of the room. He was wearing a bright yellow shirt and black chinos, nothing like the formal business attire I was expecting. He turned and rose as soon as he saw us. He seemed surprisingly young, not much older than I was.

"Harold, this is Jon Jones," said Dani.

"Yes, yes," he said, extending his hand, looking into my face eagerly. "Thank you, Dani," he said as she left.

"I have to say," he began as we sat down, "that Niccole has been a wonderful addition to our community. The children just love her."

His comment rather disarmed me. I could hardly be the inquiring reporter after such a friendly opening. "Well, she's been enjoying her work here, that's for sure."

"And I understand you are thinking of joining us?" When I gave a slight nod, he went on, "We'd love to have you. Is there anything I can tell you?"

"Well, actually, I'm wondering how hard it would be for me to adjust. For example, exactly how much work does one have to do?"

"Here, it's a minimum of 12 hours a week. At the Farm in New Hampshire, they have a 36-hour week."

"And are people paid for this work?"

"Oh yes, $12 an hour. That's set to cover room and board. If a person wants more money for other things, then he would work more—or create and sell things on the outside. And then, of course, here, most people have outside jobs. That doesn't happen at the Farm."

"Does a person get a choice of jobs? For example, if I didn't want to wash dishes. . . ?"

"Oh, yes, you get a choice in what you want to sign up for. Of course, we hope that members will step forward to fill needed tasks if there's a vacancy. On jobs that aren't too popular we have a rotation. And yes, dish washing is an example. You'd probably be expected to do a three-week shift of that every six months or so." He added matter-of-factly, "I do it. You get used to it."

"And what about my phone, and watching TV? And my computer?"

Horace looked at me with a certain firmness.

"Well, the basic idea is you come here because you want to get away from that stuff." After a pause, he continued, "Here, we allow a maximum of two hours a day. We have electronic cubicles

186 BEING HUMAN BEING

you can rent for that amount of time. In New Hampshire"—he
gave me another firm look—"they are pretty serious about it. It's
off the table. None."

Wow! I thought. That would be like diving into an icy ocean.

"And what do people do for fun?" I asked.

"I don't know whether 'fun' is the right word." He smiled.
"That's a little superficial. We're interested in happiness here,
human fulfillment. And we measure it. Many of us keep a record,
so we have some numbers to guide us as we make different
decisions on how we do things. But, to answer your question, we
have a number of activities. We have two—no, now it's three—
different dramatic groups giving plays all the time. There's no
end of crafts—woodcarving has become especially popular. And
then there's our outreach projects, like assisting selected cases of
homeless people, and Nancy's Cradle, we call it, for new mothers
in difficult circumstances." After a pause he said, "So we've got
plenty of rewarding challenges."

That seemed interesting—and quite commendable. I decided
to shift the subject.

"Horace, I've been puzzled about one thing about BHB, and
about this place. That is the secrecy, the unwillingness to be
publicly known. I mean, you don't even give this organization
here a name. Why is that?"

Horace gave me a calm, confident look. Obviously, this was
not the first time he had faced this topic.

After a careful pause, he asked, "Does Niccole have state
certification in child care?"

"Gee, I've never thought about it, but no, I'm pretty sure she
doesn't. So what does that have to do with. . . ?"

Horace said nothing, letting me think my way to his point.

"So what you're saying," I continued, "is if this community got publicity, state inspectors would come here and check on her credentials, and. . . ?"

"Take her to jail, fine her $50,000, fine us $500,000—who knows? And it's not just Niccole." A note of frustration entered his voice. "Practically everything we do here is in violation of some kind of governmental regulation, from running our own school to growing radishes on the roof, tended by child labor. What you see here—all these creative activities, gardening by children and so on—can seem when viewed from a distance by newspapers and bureaucrats—as some kind of wrong. If you wrote a story about us, we might be famous for a day or two. But then the inspectors would start showing up, and in the long run we would be destroyed as an independent, creative community."

"I guess I see," I said slowly. "Wow. I'd never really thought about that aspect of it."

"And it's not just government regulation," he continued. "All kinds of special interest groups have their finger in every pie. Liability lawyers are always cruising around ready to bring a suit for anything anyone wants to complain about—and cash in on. Manufacturers' associations set up ways to exclude newcomers and punish competitors. Unions—schoolteachers, carpenters, electricians and so forth—are always seeking to prevent anyone else from doing what they do. Hell, probably even the radish farmers have a quota, or a requirement we are not meeting."

After a few moments, he continued. "It's what we call the 'massification' of human relations. Made possible by the abuse, or at least overuse, of technology. Instead of people interacting with each other on a friendly, personal basis, you have far-off impersonal agencies making rules for people they don't know anything about."

He gave me a broad smile. "Our little community is like a chipmunk in a forest of drunken elephants. The last thing we want to do is stand up on our hind legs and shout, 'Hey, look at me!'"

He let out a deep breath and gave me a sly smile. "So that's why we'd rather you don't write about us."

"I see, I see."

"And you won't, right?" he added, with a note of concern.

"No, no, don't worry," I said. "I won't blow any whistle on you."

Shortly thereafter I rose to leave. One last question popped into my head. "By the way, do they have electricity there, in New Hampshire?"

Horace gave a patient smile, acknowledging my tone of anxiety. "Not in the cabins. I'm afraid they use kerosene lamps."

As we shook hands, he said, speaking in a firm tone but giving me a warm smile, "I'd really like to see you here, but I can see you need to think it over."

I was in rather a daze as I made it to the lobby, said goodbye to Dani, and pushed out the front door into the early evening air. My head was reeling with the different points that had come up, and I decided to walk to give myself time to digest what I had learned. It occurred to me that this meeting with Horace was probably the most significant conversation I had had in my life.

First, there was the larger historical issue that the manual community raised. Was humanity heading in the right direction with its embrace of technology? Until my recent contacts with the Nanoelectronics group, and Rebecca's group at 186th Street, I had assumed that the human race was always making progress: fire, the wheel, printing, television, space travel, and so on. More technology was better, making life easier, more productive. Over the past months, this confident assumption was increasingly being challenged. Now, after listening to Horace, I found this suspicion about technology was gelling into a fact. The advances in technology and communication lead to massive lifestyle changes that could have many unhealthy aspects.

And then there was the problem of far-off authority, the "massification" of social relations that Horace pointed to. Technology leads to ever-bigger units of production, and control by distant, impersonal agencies that regulate the life out of people. Here you had, on E. 107th Street, an admirable, inspiring community—the kind of Utopia that people have been dreaming about for centuries. Was it being praised and imitated? Not at all. Modern society with its governments, corporations, lawyers and mass media was threatening to crush it! Its only hope was to hide out of sight.

I paced along, glancing down the street, my eyes taking in the canyon of buildings lining the street. And what did all this mean for my idea of writing a book about this movement? My trip to see Wayne in Bonners Ferry revealed how diffuse the BHB movement was, without any specific leadership or program. And now, after being pledged to secrecy by Horace, my hope of making the manual community the focus of the book was also off the table. It was obvious that releasing any concrete details about the community would put them in danger. Of course, I would never do that. In fact, it occurred to me that I couldn't even mention Cliona and her flower-selling without getting her in trouble with the sales tax people. Did my whole book project have to be thrown into the dustbin?

I must have slapped a dozen lampposts in frustration as I made my way along the pavement, my brain spinning with these jarring thoughts, that damn line of poetry constantly repeating in my head, "I left them to paint a star."

Then my thinking turned to the idea of Niccole and me joining this group. I knew that the New Hampshire community was pretty primitive, but I hadn't realized until Horace explained it, how primitive. No electricity! What would that kind of thing mean for the two of us? I understood—and admired—her eagerness to undertake the New Hampshire challenge, and somehow, I felt, it would not disappoint *her*. Since the first experiments with reducing her use of the phone, she had embraced each new step away from technology with ease and enthusiasm.

But could *I* take it? I was coming to sympathize with the anti-technology idea behind the community, but maybe my psychology wasn't up to making the adjustment. It could be like a person who agrees to make a two-week fast. You might believe in it in theory, and agree that it would improve your health, but maybe after two days you can't stand it.

I finally made it home, took the elevator to the 8th floor and my door. Niccole, who was at the stove, turned to me with excitement. "And. . .?" she said, her eyes sparkling. "How was it with Horace?"

I didn't answer at first. I hung up my blazer, sat on the stool by the door and undid my shoes and set them aside. Finally, I moved to the living room, dropped into the armchair and looked up at her. "It's complicated."

She gave a big laugh. "Now you're talking the way they do!"

"There's a lot to think about. A lot." I took a deep breath. "It's an impressive group, in many ways. Very impressive." She smiled at my compliment. "But now, here's the thing," I paused, looking up at her. "I couldn't in good conscience write any kind of book, or even an article, about it." I explained the secrecy issue, how the community depended on not being exposed to the lawyers and the regulators.

"So," I concluded, "it means I just can't write about BHB and the community. They need to be kept out of the public eye." I glanced down for a moment.

"So my plans of writing a book, being an author, blah, blah are. . . just. . . ."

Niccole came and kneeled alongside me, putting her arm around my shoulder. "Surely there must be some way you could write about it," she said. "I know you'll figure out something."

26

Two days later, I finally was able to get together with Rebecca and compare notes about our respective summer adventures.

"And so how was it?" I asked as we sat down at the Tabula Rasa, our lattes steaming in front of us. "Did you see any bears?"

"No, no, of course not," she said, smiling gayly. "But"— there was excitement in her tone—"we did have a run-in with a porcupine!"

"Wow! Aren't they the things with sharp quills?"

"More than sharp. Did you know a porcupine quill has tiny, backward-facing barbs all along it, so when it goes into your skin, it wants to go deeper into your body?"

"That sounds pretty bad."

"It is, because it means that as your muscles keep moving, they work the quill deeper and deeper into the flesh. If you're an animal like a bear or a fox, and have no way of pulling the quill out, it will kill you one way or another, either with an infection or by piercing something vital. That's why these animals learn to avoid porcupines. For some reason, dogs aren't so smart."

"Do porcupines shoot quills at you?" I asked. "I think I read that somewhere."

"No, no, that's an old wives' tale. Actually, what happens, that makes it seem that way, is the porcupine flips his tail very quickly. That's what happened to Neddy—Nancy's little dog—she was one of our group." Rebecca took a quick sip of her latte.

"So anyway, Neddy comes yelping and squealing back to camp, rubbing his nose against the ground, trying to get out the quills—but of course just making it worse. Fortunately, Henry, our guide, had some tiny pliers, which he brings along just for this possibility, and Nancy held the puppy down while Henry pulled them out of his nose." Rebecca smiled. "I got one of the quills as a souvenir."

She went on to explain what she had learned about the geology of glaciers and the different rocks she found. "I brought home pieces of quartzite to put in my flower pots." She giggled. "I just *have* to go back there and do it again next summer!" she said, pushing her hands firmly on the table. Then, after a pause, she said, "And now, how about your expedition?"

"Well, I didn't see any bears either. But I got a chance to pick huckleberries!" I explained about the berry-picking expedition and the little box of jam jars I had brought home. There seemed to be no easy way to lay out the whole picture of what I learned, and didn't learn, about BHB, so I oversimplified. "I didn't find the headquarters of BHB, but I met some really nice people."

We were interrupted by the waiter who asked if we wanted anything more. When he left, Rebecca asked, speaking gently, "And how are your plans with Niccole shaping up?" She knew, from the Nanoelectronics group, about Niccole's keen interest in the manual community.

"It's getting tougher," I said. "You know, I really love that woman. I would follow her into hell. I really would!" Rebecca smiled warmly.

"But it's not as simple as that, because you have to think about months and years and their effect on your attitudes. I mean, after we'd been in hell for a while, I might have to say, 'This is too hot, I can't stand it.' So, everything would be wrecked." Rebecca gave me a sympathetic look but didn't say anything.

"And, by the way, I wouldn't at all compare the manual community to hell. I admire them, and, more and more, I'm coming to think they are on the right track about a lot of things. But the lifestyle change of moving in with them, and, especially, moving to New Hampshire, would be very, very major for me. And I don't know whether I could stand it in the long run."

"I understand what you're saying," Rebecca said. "It would involve a lot of changes."

I stared at the table, my mind sorting through images of the primitive life. "By the way, Rebecca, did you have electric lanterns on your expedition?"

She looked at me with surprise. "No. How did you guess we didn't. . . ?"

"Just intuition," I said. "So, what happened? What. . . ?"

"We used a kerosene lamp."

"And how did that work out?"

"Oh, it was lovely. Romantic really. That little flickering flame in the center of the tent sort of brought us all together. And another thing, it made me realize I shouldn't take light for granted. With electricity, you just flick a switch"—Rebecca imitated the little finger-flipping gesture. "The kerosene lamp takes attention, effort. To light it, you have to remove the glass chimney, crank up the wick, and so on. Then—Henry showed us this—every few days you have to trim the wick, to get rid of the burnt part that gives a smokey flame."

When I didn't say anything, she said, "Why did you ask?"

"Well," I said grimly, "in New Hampshire that's what they use. Kerosene lamps."

"So, what's the problem?"

I replied, "It's one thing to play with them for a few days, like you did. But how about living with them for months? I took a breath and said it slowly. "For. Ever."

Rebecca patted my hand.

"I just don't know what to do!"

"You're sounding just the way I did when I talked about my fear of bears," she said.

"What do you mean?"

"Do you plan to die never having tried living in a manual community?"

I smiled at her rephrasing the taunt about bears that had been thrown at her by her husband.

"It is this whole question of ease versus joy, remember?" She was referring to a prompt we had at an exploration about a month ago.[5] "About how you shouldn't go through life just trying for the easy way, trying not to make mistakes. Mistakes can be creative."

Responding to my grimace, she continued, energetically. "No, really! Difficulties can enrich you. They motivate you. Like Neddy getting porcupine quills. Should we have carefully kept him on a leash to prevent any kind of accident? If we had, Neddy would have missed his experiences with off-leash adventures, and we would have missed all the challenge, and everything we learned about porcupines, and so on.

---

[5] The text of this document is included in the Appendix.

"My Stephen has a joke about it," she went on. "He says, 'If you want to learn from your mistakes and become really wise, you have to make a lot of them.'" I smiled at the wisecrack.

Rebecca patted my hand. "Anyway, I know you'll do the right thing."

27

With Rebecca's words ringing in my ears, I made my way home, sitting in the nearly empty Subway car, watching the tunnel lights flash by, one after the other, as the train screeched along.

Making mistakes. . . ? Could that be a defensible theory of living? To deliberately head into a situation where you know there might be a problem? That was an argument for taking up this challenge of going to the Farm. But I still had the problem of how could I write about what I learned and not expose them?

Then it hit me, like the pieces of a giant puzzle coming together. In writing this book about the Farm and BHB, I didn't have to be a *reporter*, and name the people and places involved. I could be a diarist. I could write a memoir about what happened to *me*, what I felt, what it was like to go back in time 100 years and live in a primitive community. I wouldn't identify the Farm or give it away. I could just say that it was "somewhere in the northeastern U.S." In fact, disguising and hiding its identity would add to the intrigue and excitement of the book!

And it wouldn't matter how the experience played out. Say the New Hampshire project turned out to be unpleasant, painful. Well, this would be an interesting experience. I certainly would have learned something, something I could tell the world about. It would be like being a travel writer going to a difficult foreign country to live for a year. You go to Uzbekistan, encounter lots of ugly, unpleasant customs. You have to eat ants, dry yourself with goat skins, and so on. Not fun, but still, when you come home you have an interesting book to write about your experiences!

The same idea could apply to New Hampshire: it would make an excellent subject for a book, however it turned out. I would describe what my life was like living for one full year in a primitive community. If it worked out well, then the book would recount how great it was. If it didn't, then that would be a great story, too, detailing the problems—and the pain, and why their theories of simple living are wrong.

If, for example, they made me do all my writing with pencil and paper, and this proved interesting and energizing, then I would report that. If hoeing corn all day gave me a feeling of contentment, I would say so. If it left me frustrated and morose, then I could report that. I started to imagine the beginning lines of this sad chapter: "The dark clouds pressed ominously against the wooded hills as I zipped my jacket against the rain and took up my hoe."

This was a win-win opportunity for an author!

I started turning over possible titles in my mind. If primitive living proved to be a positive experience, one that showed escaping from the technology-gripped world left us happier and more creative, I could call it something like *Human Liberation*. Or, if a touch of wisecracking seemed right, maybe *Joy of Lamplight*.

If it turned out badly, if reducing dependence on modern inventions turned out to be frustrating and painful, then a good title might be *Fighting Progress—and Losing*. If I wanted to strike a light-hearted tone, then maybe *Burned by Kerosene*.

I hadn't realized until that moment how discouraged I had

become as a result of the collapse of my planned BHB book project. I had worked myself into a dream of becoming a successful author, and then that dream had been crushed. Now this challenge was back, and in terms that seemed to guarantee success. No matter what happened, I would be able to write an important book on the experience that Davidson and Small would be sure to take!

I could hardly wait to get back to Niccole. I didn't quite run along 47th Street after I made it out of the Subway station, but I was certainly race-walking.

When I burst into the bedroom, I found her reading in bed, propped up with pillows, the light of the lamp shining against her hair. I knelt down beside the bed, took her arm and rubbed my head against it. She smiled at my enthusiasm and tickling.

"What on earth has got into you!?"

"I've figured it all out! We can go to New Hampshire. In fact, we *have* to go to New Hampshire!"

I explained to her my theory of writing a book about our experiences, however they turned out. "I think the world would want to know what it's like to seriously cut back on technology, to emphasize manual work and social relationships."

Niccole was having trouble digesting my sudden willingness to embrace the manual community idea.

"So you think we should go to New Hampshire?"

"Yes. Yes."

"And stay there for. . .?"

"My idea is for a year. No matter how bad it is, we stick it out for a year. I'll need at least that much to write an authoritative book on what the BHB philosophy really amounts to."

A glowing smile came over her face. Now she understood my enthusiasm. "Really?!" she exclaimed. She grabbed my head with both hands. We kissed, hard.

I went to the kitchen and sat down at the table to write out some possible book titles, and sketch a chapter outline.

A few minutes later, Niccole came from the bedroom, walking slowly. There was a frown on her face. "What about the problem of not being able to identify them? How can you write about the New Hampshire community if you can't reveal the name?"

"Oh, I've thought about that. I'll give it a fictitious name and disguise the location to protect it from the regulators."

She was silent a moment. "Will that be enough?"

"What do you mean?"

"Well, if your name is on the book, the regulators or the FBI or someone will come and force you to reveal everything. You can be forced to testify—that happened to Linus, one of our managers at Everett, in a court case. There was a suit about someone falling off one of our chairs. Linus didn't want to have anything to do with it but he got a subpoena thing. He was forced to testify in court."

As soon as she said it, I realized she was right. Any book I wrote on the Farm could contain many actionable revelations, points about child labor, about drinking unpasteurized milk, selling turnips without sales taxes, and who knows what else? With my name on the cover, I could end up in court—forced to identify the place and the people involved. I looked up in consternation.

Then a thought cut through the haze. "Hey! My name doesn't have to be on the cover!"

Niccole gave a puzzled frown.

"I can use a pen name!" Her frown turned to a broad smile.

"All kinds of famous authors do that," I continued. "Like Mark Twain."

Niccole stared at me. "Brilliant!" she said. "I knew you'd figure out the answer." She kissed my forehead and went back into the bedroom.

What name should it be? I took a paper clip in my fingers and twiddled with it. 'Mark somebody'? That was a little obvious, but I liked the firm authority of it. A person makes his Mark on the world. Yes, I should pick a name that gets attention and conveys authority. I turned the problem over in my mind. How about Power, or Powers. Yes, 'David Powers' sounded good.

As I sat there twisting the paper clip, my vision resting on the green blotter, a disturbing thought entered my mind. With authors like Mark Twain, the pen name was part of their fame. Everyone knew he was Samuel Clemens, and where to find him. In fact, he was even given an honorary degree at Oxford. In my case, the purpose of a pen name would be to hide me from the world. Forever! I couldn't go walking down the street telling people I was David Powers. The publisher would have to promise not to release my name. Niccole would know, but no one else. Not even my dad. If he knew, he wouldn't be able to resist telling all his friends that the famous author David Powers was really his son, and within a week there'd be an FBI agent at my door with a subpoena.

The paper clip in my fingers became more twisted. I began to see what was behind my feeling of dismay. I had held in the back of my mind, since my first success as a writer in the third grade, the idea that I was going to be a famous author. That was the underlying aim. When my father taunted me about my lack of success, this ambition, this expectation of being a famous author, was my secret ace in the hole. Now, when at last I had a book project that promised to bring this dream to fruition, I couldn't put my name on it! The crowds would be surging down 5th Avenue praising David Powers's famous book and I would be a bystander, lonely and ignored.

What a cruel joke.

But. . . but. . . I began to sense that maybe something was missing in the way I was looking at things, this emphasis on fame. After all, is fame a healthy ambition? Maybe third-grade children think it is, but aren't we supposed to outgrow childish impulses? I looked at the ceiling, my brow furrowed. I felt I was figuring out something new, something important.

My thoughts turned to my father and the way he defined success.

Wasn't this at the core of the tension between us? He prized material measures of success: money and fame. Wasn't it time for me to rise beyond this kind of third-grade thinking?

I took a deep breath, looked around at the walls. I started understanding the whole problem more and more clearly: Being focused on fame was childish!

But if getting famous shouldn't be the purpose of writing, what was? Maybe there were a lot of answers here. The purpose of my writing at Ringo was to inform real estate shoppers, that is, to pass along data. That's a legitimate—if not very exciting—activity. And then there are all kinds of playwrights and novelists who aim to entertain and amuse, to tell stories. Which is fine.

But that wasn't what was attracting me to figuring out BHB

and writing about the Farm. What was happening—it suddenly became quite clear to me—is that *I was looking for answers to questions, and wanted to tell others what I found out.* Is turning away from technology possible? Do we end up happier if we do? I was curious.

I sat there for several more minutes pondering this new conception about who I really was. What was motivating me as a writer was curiosity, the excitement of figuring out something and telling people what I was discovering. Fame was unimportant, maybe even a little hollow. Writing a book about the Farm would be just as much fun no matter what author's name was on the cover.

I took a long, deep breath of satisfaction. In a matter of minutes, I felt I had suddenly grown 20 years older and wiser. I tossed the twisted paper clip into the wastebasket and rushed into the bedroom.

Niccole was lying on the bed by the lamp, reading. I jumped onto the bed beside her, and swung my arm out with a bit of drama.

"I've finally figured it out!" I said, looking intently into her eyes.

She smiled, the patient mother indulging the excitable child.

I spaced the words out carefully. "The measure of a good writer is not how famous he is but what he discovers!"

"Hmmm," she said, smiling. She gently pressed her fingertip on my nose. "That sounds like a quotation from somebody famous."

28

Two days later, we did the formal proposal of marriage, an event that took both of us a little by surprise. In fact, you could say Niccole's mother triggered the action.

Niccole was making her regular Friday morning call to Edith when she called me into the bedroom.

"Jon, Mom can't use the cell phone Rick gave her. Can you work her through it?" Niccole handed me the phone. I gathered that this was the Rick who had coached us in pickleball that afternoon.

"Hi, Edith, how are you?"

"Oh, Jon, it's so good to hear your voice. This is just terrible! Rick left me this phone, so I could reach him when he's driving." She lowered her voice and said, "We're meeting for lunch"—there was a mixture of guilt and pride in her tone—"and I have to tell him where I made the reservation. But I can't turn this silly thing on. He told me how, but I guess I've forgotten."

I asked her to describe the phone and got her to locate the thin white button on the side, and she pressed it.

"Yes, that's it!"—I had to take my ear away from the phone, her voice was so loud. "Now it's all lit up and I can go ahead. Thank you, thank you, thank you!"

After she calmed down, she asked, "And how are you and Niccole doing?"

"Fine, fine."

"I mean, are you, well, I mean, getting toward being serious?" My. . . she's been reading our minds, I thought.

"Well, uh. . ."

"I've been thinking a lot about you. What I want to say is that if you and Niccole decide to go ahead, I couldn't imagine a more perfect son-in-law. I mean that!"

"That's. . . that's very kind of you, Edith. Yes. . . well. . . let me give you back to Niccole."

While Niccole was finishing up her call, I thought hard about Edith's nudge. It probably was time for us to announce plans.

After a few more minutes, Niccole hung up and came into the kitchen.

I said, "She's right."

"Oh, so Mom was onto you about it too?" I nodded. We were both silent.

"There is one thing." I paused. "If—after this one year at the Farm—if I was unable to handle it and you wanted to stay. . .?"

"Oh we would make it work. That's the whole idea of BHB, you know, compromise. You may not have understood that."

"What do you mean?"

"It's not that there's one right way." Niccole had adopted a serious tone. "Everyone is supposed to explore, to try things one way, and then another. In fact, I guess you didn't know, but at the Farm, after you've been there three years, you're actually required to leave it for a period. That's so you can make a real comparison—and come back with new ideas. You have to make a positive decision if you want to come back."

"Wow. I didn't know about that."

"And even on their practices, they don't insist. It's a recommendation. They want you to make a serious effort to try a thing, but, if after that you say it doesn't work for you, then you work out an arrangement. For example, they do have electric power at the barn—to run the refrigerator to keep the milk cold."

"Really?"

"Yes. So, if you said that—after trying them—you couldn't stand kerosene lamps, they would probably be open to an adjustment."

"Okay, yes, I see."

"But what about you and me? What if you wanted kerosene and I didn't?"

"Jon!" she cried out, giving me a firm look. "Where have you been? That's what marriage is all about: working things out. If you want potatoes for supper and I want carrots, we work it out. That's what we've been doing all along, for months."

I saw she had a point. I'd been a little overreacting to the possibility of a conflict between us about adjusting to less technology. Niccole and I already worked well as a couple.

"Well, okay then, it looks like it's sort of settled," I said. "We should get married and go to New Hampshire."

Niccole beamed at me but remained silent, with an expectant look.

"Okay, okay," I said. "You want me to officially propose?" She nodded, and to accentuate the point, tapped her index finger twice on her nose, signaling "correct!" as if we were playing a game of charades.

"I guess we should do this in a low-tech, old-fashioned way," I said. Niccole giggled at my teasing allusion to BHB.

I got down on my knees beside the bed and looked into her beaming, expectant eyes. "Niccole Evenson," I said, adopting a pompous tone, "I hereby extend to you my official proposal of marriage. Will you—no, *wilt thou*—marry me?"

She leaned toward me, and, playing games with my use of formal language, adopted a stagy slang, "Yea, man!" We hugged hard.

"You know," I said a few moments later, as we were lying together on the bed, "I suppose you could consider getting into marriage a kind of spring." She nodded. "It's jumping into a new thing." Then I added, "And it's kind of low tech." She snuggled against my ribs.

"And then, of course," I continued, "we're also going off to New Hampshire. I wonder if there's such a thing as a double spring?"

"If there isn't, then we just invented it."

After a few more minutes of caressing, she sat up and said, "Wouldn't it be neat if the marriage ceremony could be a spring, too, a real BHB spring. Something that steps back in technology. I mean, it shouldn't be an ordinary wedding. What do you think?"

I thought for a moment about this novel idea. "Maybe I could place a wooden wedding ring on your finger?"

"Well, that's an interesting idea," she said, smiling. "But I'm afraid it wouldn't hold up very well when I washed the dishes."

She gave me a wink. "I'll think of something."

29

After our engagement in early September, to give ourselves time, we set the marriage date for January 2nd. "To start the year off right" as Niccole confidently put it. The week after that we would move into the manual community on 107th Street, and then, assuming we passed the trial period, we would head to the Farm in early April. Everybody said that was the best time to go, since that was when they started the vegetable gardens up there.

The many weeks of preparation involved quite a bit more stress than I had anticipated. It's one thing to say you're going to step into a bright new future, but doing it isn't so easy. Maybe in novels the hero just walks into the sunset, but in the real world, people have responsibilities and connections to unwind. In our case, we had jobs to leave and an apartment to close.

Asher was very much behind our project to join the BHB community, and we worked out a way for me to continue to work part time at Ringo Listings while Niccole and I stayed at 107th Street. I would help train a replacement to take my place when I left for New Hampshire in April.

I had a big struggle dealing with the stuff in the apartment. Beyond some bare bones housewares that we would take with us to 107th Street, everything else had to go. Isn't it strange how hard it is to throw things away? A set of dinner plates with the picture of Eiffel Tower, never used. A pair of aluminum rock-climbing carabiners, of course, never used. And so forth.

The biggest challenge was the filing cabinet of my writings drafts and research materials, most of which had to do with *Prisoner of Love.* I agonized for days about what to do with all this material. I tried going through it trying to save a little bit of the more promising parts, but I found this was absurdly time-consuming. Starting on the first folder, I found myself reading each item, thinking about it, seeing some value in it, debating which pile to put it in. After 20 minutes, I hadn't even dealt with 1/50th of it.

I considered the idea of putting the filing cabinet in storage somewhere. But aside from the cost, I realized this was just putting off the job of selection that I lacked the time and energy to attempt. And why, I asked, would I have more time and energy to go through these papers page by page 10 or 20 years from now?

I finally decided to grasp the bull by the horns. One morning when I was alone in the apartment—I saw no reason to burden Niccole with this personal decision—I made four trips to the trash bin in the basement, carrying one file drawer down in the elevator each trip. After dumping out the last drawer, I stepped back, surveyed this mound of human creativity and made the sign of the cross.

In the elevator on my way back up to the apartment, I experienced a surprising change of mood. Throughout the process of throwing these materials away I had been understandably grim. After all, I was physically documenting the pointlessness of years of creative efforts. One would expect that at the completion of this act my mood should have hit rock bottom.

But no! As the elevator started to rise and the vision of the paper clumps left behind in the trash bin flashed through my mind, I sensed a powerful feeling of liberation. I was not the possessor of all those endlessly revised chapters of *Prisoner of Love* and so forth, duty-bound to rewrite and remarket this material to the end of time. That was now history, gone forever. I was free, free to discover new worlds and write about them.

Niccole was, of course, going through this same kind of struggle, paring down her possessions. Like me, she understood this was a task no one else could help with, so we didn't talk about it. One Saturday morning, as she was twisting out through the front door of the apartment with an armload of dresses and sweaters, she said loudly to nobody in particular, "Why? Why? Why do I have so many clothes!"

Amidst our struggles with details of moving, we carried on our happy engagement. During one of our regular Thursday evening suppers at Il Giorno, after the plates had been cleared and we were waiting for our one tiramisu (we split this sublime dish), Niccole looked up and said, "I've been thinking about where we should have the wedding."

"And. . . ?"

She smiled broadly. "Bear Mountain!"

I immediately saw it was right. "Of course. You could say that's where our romance began."

Niccole leaned toward me in excitement, saying, "And. . . ." She let the suspense build.

"Yes?"

"I was talking with Cliona about it, and—do you know?—she has performed Celtic wedding ceremonies for people, and she said she would be willing to do one for us!"

"That seems like a neat idea," I said. "Of course, remember that on January 2nd Bear Mountain is going to be cold and full of snow. There could even be a blizzard. It could get pretty dicey."

"Oh, right," she replied. "That's why I've been thinking of a very short ceremony. And I don't think we should try to get to the top of the mountain. Actually, I wanted to do it beside Bear Mountain Lake."

I said I thought that sounded like a good idea.

Niccole continued, "I'm afraid Mom won't be able to make the trip, because of her health. I asked her about it yesterday when I explained about my idea of Bear Mountain. She says she can ride in a car only about 20 minutes before the nausea sets in. She did insist, however, that we had to go to Warren as soon as we could after the ceremony for what she called 'the wedding banquet.' Knowing her, it's going to be quite a production."

"Of course, we'll go. That would make her very happy."

There was a pause in our conversation. We were thinking about the same thing: my parents. We both sensed there was too much distance, physically and emotionally, to invite them to attend the ceremony, especially such a non-traditional one.

Niccole said, her voice quiet, tentative, "Could we go visit your parents sometime later, after the wedding? I mean, it's too informal, this little service, to invite them up here."

I was pretty sure my parents would be pleased to see me married, and also that they would approve of Niccole. The problem was telling my father, who was so success-oriented, about our project of dropping out of the modern, commercial world and going to New Hampshire.

"I suppose we ought to go see them," I said. "Mom certainly will want to meet you. It's just that I don't know how to explain to my dad our going to the Farm. To him, it's going to seem like we're becoming shiftless hippies, turning our backs on the world of modern production and prosperity." After a pause, I said, "Of course, we could let them assume that we were continuing with our current jobs, and keep the whole New Hampshire thing a secret. But that would involve deception, and I don't think. . . ."

"Well, of course not. But, Jon," she was speaking earnestly, "you have nothing to be ashamed of. This New Hampshire project, like you say, is an opportunity. I'll tell him—if you don't—that this is a career opening. That you're a brilliant writer, and that you are preparing a major work on the most publicized issue in the modern world."

Niccole gave me a triumphant grin. "I'll tell him he has a son he can really be proud of!"

Her words opened a new perspective for me, a new way of viewing my father's judgmental attitude. Maybe Niccole could convince him that I was a more promising personality than he had assumed. But whether she did or not, her words gave me a new confidence. If my father wanted to criticize my career choices, well, now I saw that should be considered as just one man's opinion. I felt I had outgrown being my father's 'son.'

We decided to make plans to go to Orlando in February.

30

The first thing we saw as we pulled up to Hessian Lake at Bear Mountain were the skaters, dozens of them enjoying the broad sheet of ice that covered the lake. There were moms holding the hands of toddlers whose ankles flopped sideways as they flailed and scraped along the ice, and several young women figure skaters working on very professional-looking spins and jumps. An older man in a red jacket, on hockey skates, tracked a large circle, leaning forward, chin jutting out, hands clasped behind, each foot methodically crossing over in front of the other as he curved around.

The sky was overcast, but the cloud layer was high—we could clearly see the ridge of the mountains above the lake. It was below freezing, but there was little wind so it didn't feel too cold. Better than average conditions for a January wedding ceremony, I thought.

Asher had brought Niccole, Cliona, and me in his car and we were the first of the wedding party to arrive. We got out to explore. We were dressed warmly, with boots and heavy coats, though we didn't expect to have to endure the cold for long. Niccole and Cliona assured us that their prepared ceremony was going to be very short.

While waiting for the rest of the party from the Community to arrive, we walked to the lake and onto the ice. Niccole did a little running slide, throwing her arms out wide in her full-length tan overcoat. "This is neat!" she cried out, twisting around. "You know," she said, walking back toward Asher and me—Cliona had stayed on the shore—"maybe we could have the wedding out here?"

I think she was mainly teasing, but there was an element of seriousness in her tone.

I looked at Asher. He gave her a fatherly smile. "Well, it probably would be the first wedding in history performed on ice."

I grinned. "But then people would say our marriage started on thin ice."

Niccole giggled at my jest, and came back with one of her own. "Or that we had a slippery beginning."

At that moment, a great cracking sound came from the ice, almost like a thunderclap. Niccole gave a shriek and grabbed my arm. "It's breaking! Oh, my God, how scary! We didn't even think to test the ice!" She dragged me toward the shore 20 feet away. Soon we were back on the land with Cliona.

"Well, that was one really dumb idea," Niccole said, surveying the frozen surface. Then she asked, pointing at the skaters who were twirling and scuffling out on the ice just as before, "Aren't they afraid? Shouldn't they get off if it's breaking?"

Asher smiled at her. "Ice does that all the time. In fact, it's a sign that you have very thick ice. What's happening is the ice expands and presses with great force, sideways against itself. That's what forms those big fracture lines, like that one there," he pointed to a long crack on the ice in front of us.

"Well, anyway," said Niccole, "I think this marriage ought to begin on solid ground." She gave me a wink and then an excited hug. "In fact, right here, where we're standing is a wonderful place. Don't you think, Cliona?"

"Yes, it's perfect," she replied, "and I'll stand over here"—she pointed—"and you two can face the lake and the mountain beyond."

While we were waiting for the others, Niccole happened to comment, waving her arm toward the lake and the trees, "Oh, it's so wonderful getting back to nature like this!"

These words reminded me of the comment Asher made many months ago, explaining why he moved Ringo Listings to the building alongside Tomkins Square, with its grass and trees. Something about 'getting back to nature,' he had said. At the time, I took it as a wisecrack, and assumed that the real reason for the move had to do with the cost of the lease. Now that I knew more about Asher, and his connection with BHB, I realized that this business of moving toward nature, however slight and symbolic, could have been intentional. I turned to him.

"That was a spark! Right?"

Asher looked at me with curiosity.

"Our moving to Tompkins Square. That was a spark—well, maybe a spring, because you got the benefit, too. Right?" I said, looking into his eyes.

His grin broadened to a knowing smile, but he didn't say anything.

"Wow!" My brow furrowed. "Do you realize that move made possible everything that has happened to me over the past year!" I looked around at the lake and then into Niccole's eyes. "I would never have met this lady here"—I nodded toward her—"never have learned about BHB, never have gone to Idaho, or to New

Hampshire." I kept shaking my head. "Wow! Wow! Wow!"

"What are you talking about?" asked Niccole, with a perplexed smile. "What made what possible?"

I smiled at Asher and he smiled back. I grabbed Niccole, gave her a hug and looked into her eyes. "It's complicated." We both laughed.

I turned back to Asher. "And what a hell of a spark that was! A miracle, really. It completely changed our lives."

"You give me too much credit, my boy," he replied, laughing gently. "Actually, we were pushed out of the old place for a building remodel. Tompkins Square was just next on the list. It was only after we moved that I realized you could say we were getting back to nature—a tiny bit."

After a pause, he looked at me firmly and said, "Miracles come from the soul of the universe. All we can do is to open our eyes and notice them."

He gave me an affectionate pat on the back. I looked up and took a deep breath. At that moment, everything my eyes saw, the sweeping gray skies encircling the rounded hilltops, seemed miraculous.

Soon the two other cars of the wedding party arrived, carrying Elle and three other women, friends of Niccole's from the community, along with two husbands. So, we were a party of 10 altogether.

After introductions and handshaking, Cliona took her position facing all of us, her back to the lake. She looked quite priestly and impressive in her dark purple woolen overcoat. Niccole and I stepped forward to face her.

She began the ceremony ringing a tiny silver bell which made a delightful tinkling. Niccole leaned against me and whispered, "It's to ward off any bad spirits."

Then Cliona invited us to say our "tributes," which were declarations of why we loved our mate. We had written out (and more or less memorized) our tributes, but decided to keep them secret from each other until this wedding day.

I went first. Looking into Niccole's eyes, I declared, "Niccole, I love you for your courage and enthusiasm. When there's a challenge, a task, or a voyage—or thin ice, (I ad-libbed)—you're ready to try it. And I love your sparkling eyes." Her face lit up with a huge smile.

It took her a few minutes to calm down. She drew out a handkerchief and blew her nose, took a deep breath and read her tribute. "Jon, I love you because you are so patient and thoughtful, always asking questions. You understand everything before everyone else does. That makes you the wisest person I know. Most of all, I love knowing that, with you–and perhaps because of you, whatever lies ahead will always be filled with adventure and new discoveries."

As I thought about her words, then and since, I knew that her compliment about my brain wasn't, objectively speaking, particularly accurate. I'm not really wise, or even very smart. But the fact that she feels that I am does give me confidence. At least, I tell myself, there's one person in the world who truly believes in me.

The service continued with my slipping the wedding ring on Niccole's finger. We had decided against wood (!), but had vetoed any jewels. Niccole's was a silver ring with a delicate Celtic design.

The last ritual was jumping the broom, which I gathered

symbolized the couple's starting to keep house together. The object Cliona unwrapped for this purpose wasn't any ordinary, store-bought broom. It was made of twigs tied together at the end of a stick. Though medieval in character, it was newly-made: I could see a few dead leaves still clinging to the twigs. Who made it, I wondered, and where? It certainly didn't come from the concrete corridors of New York City.

The jumping part was more of a challenge than it might seem. Yes, Cliona laid the broom down on the ground nearly flat, propping the handle end up slightly on a little block of wood. But remember, we were wearing boots, and in snow. Also, as Niccole explained to me the night before, when we had practiced going through the ceremony, you had to jump across, not step or walk, together. By carefully counting to three out loud we made the jump successfully, earning enthusiastic applause and cheering from our fans.

Cliona concluded the service reading a Celtic blessing. The words seemed especially significant for a couple planning to redirect their lives toward manual labors. When Niccole took up calligraphy a few months later, this document was one of the first things she copied out. We framed it and hung it on the wall.

May the light of your soul guide you.
May the light of your soul bless the work that you do with the secret love and warmth of your heart.
May you see in what you do the beauty of your own soul.
May the sacredness of your work bring healing, light and renewal to those who work with you and to those who see and receive your work.

May your work never weary you.
May it release within you wellsprings of refreshment,
inspiration and excitement.

After the ceremony, we drove to the Abbey Inn in Peekskill, where Elle had arranged for our wedding banquet. It was an impressive building, fronted with rough stonework and a medieval-looking tower. It even had a tiny stone cross at the peak of the roof, reminiscent of a monastery. Our private dining room had a large table, its dark oak top at least two inches thick. When we walked in, there were already presents piled at Niccole's place.

Elle tapped on her wine glass with a spoon. "Let's have Cliona start with grace, then we won't have to worry about who starts when." Cliona obliged with a few thoughtful words, and we all sat down, Niccole on my left, Asher on my right.

Amidst the general chattering, wine-serving and order-taking, Niccole began opening the presents. The first—from Elle—was a hand-operated coffee-bean grinder. "Oh, this is wonderful," said Niccole. "Now I can make real coffee in the morning!" The most impressive gift, I thought, was a little necklace of tiny dark blue beads from Cliona. Niccole beamed after I fastened it around her neck. We sensed its Celtic mystic significance, and it matched her cream-colored sweater very well.

"Yes," Elle was saying to the couples at the end of the table, "I thought of that out at the lake, too." They were smiling and nodding, sharing some engrossing topic.

"What... what is this?" Niccole asked.

"Oh, it's about this play," Elle said. She turned and gestured to Linda, "this amazing play written by the amazing son of this amazing mother!" Linda beamed politely. "Tell them about it," Elle continued, gesturing toward Asher and me.

"Well," said Linda, "Braydon—our son—has written a little play that was performed this week. It's about this young woman, Lisa, who accidentally takes a 'negativity pill', thinking it's her vitamin pill." The others at the table—who had seen this drama performed at the community—laughed knowingly.

"This pill makes her say no to everything. A waiter asks if she wants coffee and she says no, when she actually does. Her mother asks her if she wants an umbrella when she's going out into the pouring rain, and she says no, and so on. Anyway"— Linda paused and took a quick sip of wine—"Anyway, she goes to this doctor, a famous, wise doctor with a big beard and a German accent. After thinking long and hard, he tells her to take a second 'negativity pill' to counteract the first one. His theory was to take advantage of the idea that a minus times a minus is a plus. So, the second pill should cancel the effect of the first.

"Well"—Linda paused and looked around the table, enjoying a moment of suspense—"his theory wasn't quite right. Instead of getting rid of the 'no's,' the pill makes her add another 'no' to everything she says. So, she ends up speaking in double negatives. That's the title of the play: *Double Negative*.

"So, that's why we thought of you and Niccole up there at the lake"—Linda nodded toward us—"because the play ends with a wedding ceremony, with this character, Lisa, saying to the minister, 'I solemnly swear that I do not, not take this man to be my lawfully wedded husband.'"

Everyone laughed heartily, especially Niccole, who said to the group, with her hand on my shoulder, "Well, I do *not, not* love this man!" Then she turned and kissed me hard. Elle's husband pounded on the table, saying "Here, here!"

Some minutes later, as I was enjoying the animated conversation and basking in the camaraderie of the group, a thought crossed my mind: there were no phones here! No one was peeking down under the table, no one had stepped away to tap and swipe. In fact, I was pretty sure that no one even had a phone on their person. They were, so to speak, 100% present, with nothing to distract their energy and attention from those around them.

Except me. Yes, I had turned my phone off. But I was still aware of it. It was attracting a tiny fraction of my awareness, compelling a connection to the outside world. It was preventing me from fully joining my human circle.

And then, for the first time in my life, it hit me that I didn't like this feeling of distraction. I wanted to be 100% connected with Niccole, and Elle, and Cliona, and the energetic, creative people in this room. I didn't want even one corner of my mind drawn to the clatter of the outside world.

I turned to Asher and quietly said, "Excuse me a second." I got up and walked to the coat room, found my wool overcoat and slipped my phone into one of its pockets. I came back to the dining room and resumed my seat.

"Feeling better?" Asher asked with a smile.

I was pretty sure that he knew what I had done. As I'd learned over the years, Asher is a very savvy guy. Of course, his reasoning was assisted by the fact that I had not been gone long enough to have visited the men's room.

I thought about his question for a few moments. I glanced

at Niccole—who smiled back at me. I let my gaze swing around the table, looking at each face, letting the idea sink in that, now, I was giving each person all of my attention. It gave me a feeling of centeredness, of completeness.

I turned back to Asher. "Yes," I said, "Much better. More human, actually."

"Good for you," he said, smiling broadly.

It wasn't until a few minutes later that it dawned on me that this little exercise of putting aside the phone said something about how I would react to the New Hampshire project. Until now, I had viewed the idea of leaving behind technology rather negatively. I assumed that it would be an unpleasant burden, like having to eat broccoli, which Mom always said was good for me, but was not something I ever looked forward to. I had viewed going to the Farm as a necessary duty. It was a task I had to carry out, a job of information-collecting as an author. Now, all of a sudden, the Farm had an appeal to me. It was something I was looking forward to.

I pressed Niccole's thigh under the table. She turned and gave me a cheerful, questioning look.

"Hey," I said quietly. "I just realized something."

She looked at me expectantly.

I said, slowly and carefully, "I might actually enjoy the Farm. In fact,"—I let the moment of drama build—"I might be happier there than I am in New York City."

She giggled and gave my cheek a delicate pinch. "Of course, you will be!"

Appendix

BHB exploration prompts mentioned in the text

1. Electronic Distractions and Time for Living

There really aren't 24 hours in a day, not in a human day. We use up most of those hours in fairly blank activities including sleeping, resting, cooking, eating, dressing, chores, moving from place to place, and heck, just picking up things we drop. And if we work in a mechanical job, there's 6-10 more hours gone. That leaves us with something like 6 hours a day for real connections with children, family and friends, and for engaging in the creative challenges that strengthen our community and give deeper meaning to life.

Well, 6 hours a day is what we spend on electronic distractions these days.

A century ago, before electronics hit us, people had those 6 hours for dinner parties, for active participation in games and sports, music and drama. For guiding children to identify songbirds. Don't we want to restore this social vitality!?

BHB

2. The Power of Boredom

The human brain naturally seeks stimulation. Sitting alone in the forest, we are impelled to rise up to explore, to challenge, and to connect with others.

225

Now someone invents an anti-boredom machine, an electronic device that will provide stimulation. You sit all day, impelled to tap on it, lured by games, fragmentary contacts with electronic others, and titillating glimpses of distant disasters.

The predicted consequence of this invention would be a collapse of human social connections. We would see a decline of the community organizations that supply services and help others. We would see the disappearance of social games, clubs, and worship organizations. In this new world of the electronically unbored, youths no longer climb mountains, friends don't help neighbors repair homes. Frustration and unhappiness surge.

BHB

3. Humility

Monkeys play in the trees, throwing banana peels at each other, squealing with delight.

Then comes the gift of language. Words. Words to refer to other bands of monkeys living beyond the mountains. Words to refer to vague gods high in the sky. Language, the foundation of superstition.

Will these creatures recognize their limited understanding of these far-off entities? Or will these symbols give them certainty? Will they come to fear and hate the far-off tribes they can now name with words, and make war upon them?

Will they come to believe that mysteries of creation, the mysteries of suffering and deliverance, are controlled by gods they can now name, governments whose commands are written down in heavy books: obey or be slayed!

To be saved from woe, the monkeys need the gift of humility to temper the gift of words. To learn to say, with each word that signals a vast, far-off world, "Here's what I think, but I could be wrong."

BHB

4. Ease or Joy?
The Choice between Technology and Humanity

In the beginning, human beings are savages, foraging as animals, knowing nothing of beauty. No one asks, "Where did the stars come from?"

Technology liberates them, opening a vast universe of ideas and creativity. But technology doesn't stop advancing. Machines create a world where nothing can go wrong, where every want is satisfied. These physical gifts—of ease and entertainment—can undermine joy. We could end up as blobs of protoplasm on couches, our every need filled by wires, tubes and screens. Electrons dancing on glass distract from children, block thoughtful arguments, and ward off lovers. We end up unchallenged, bored and depressed. Unhappy. Reaching for sugar, for alcohol, for drugs. Indirectly—and directly—choosing death over life.

Without thoughtful intervention, the human race may go through a long cycle, from brutish, suffering emptiness tens of thousands of years ago, to a fairly high degree of liberation. Then, at a turning point around 1900-1950 CE, we begin to sink into a life of ease and electronic distraction where work, human connection—and joy—slip away. Few stop to look at the heavens, amazed.

To avoid this tragic cycle, humans need to explore how to put technology in its place, how to make it an aid to human creativity and flourishing, and not become its sad slaves.

BHB

5. Time to Think

Human communities suffer in the grip of many harmful customs and superstitions.

To overcome these errors, we need to engage in extended periods of thoughtful analysis, including careful research, searching conversations, attentive reading, attentive writing, and undistracted contemplation. On a walk in the woods, you ponder and refine views on ethics, politics and society.

Processes of analysis and rethinking can be blocked by the overuse of technologies that feature shallow entertainment, addictive mental distractions, fragmentary images, and partisan propaganda.

These trivializing, distracting technologies can prevent us from liberating ourselves. If on a walk in the woods, your mind is on your smartphone, you are unlikely to overcome the superstitions that retard your flourishing.

BHB